An Old-Fashioned Girl's Adventures in the Modern World of Dating
By April E. Bivens

An Old-Fashioned Girl's Adventures in the Modern World of Dating

An Old-Fashioned Girl's Adventures in the Modern World of Dating

ISBN-13: 978-0692740132 (April E. Bivens)
ISBN-10: 0692740139

Edited by John McCullough
Cover art and design by Jamie Rachal

Dedication and Acknowledgements

This book is dedicated to my father, Isaac Homer Bivens. I hope you are proud of me Daddy. Continue to rest in peace. It is also dedicated to those of you who still believe in a happily ever after. I will never give up on love. I love, love!!

This book would not have been possible without my editor, John McCullough. I thank you with all my heart for agreeing to be my editor. You are the best there is, and I thank you not just for your time, effort and dedication, but for coming up with the title of this book. You are a Godsend, and to you I am forever grateful. Let's get ready for the ride! It is just beginning!

A special thank you to Felicia Pinkney for her editing expertise. You are a lifesaver, and I thank God for placing us together as roommates in college.

I am forever thankful to Demetria Wideman. You have been so supportive of me. Every time I picked up the phone to ask for your opinion about minor changes to the book, and most importantly the cover – you were so helpful, and willing to assist. The dynamic duo lives on!

I am also extremely grateful for Jamie Rachal, who provided art direction for this book. Thank you Jamie for your creativity and for bringing my vision to life graphically on the cover.

A special thank you to my focus group and all of the wonderful feedback you provided before the book was published:

Tiki Cain-Collins	Niki Tinsley-Harland
Felicia Pinkney	Alduan Tartt
Lateef Ashekun	Crystal Stephens
Sandra Anderson	Demetria Wideman

An Old-Fashioned Girl's Adventures in the Modern World of Dating

Thank you to all my social media marketers — you rock! I appreciate your support in spreading the word about my book. Your kind words, and overwhelming support will always be treasured.

Jennifer Morris Coffee	Jamie Rachal
Demetria Wideman	Niki Tinsley-Harland
Dorian Newkirk	Geri Davis
Karen Ellis	Bridget Biagas
Diane Robles	Nicole Henry
Felicia Pinkney	Robin Lansing Tims
Barry Jerome Nelson	Isis Dalion
Tiki Cain-Collins	Torri Buckles
Rolandria Boyce	Jamal Woodson
Kristie Carter Gutierrez	Sydni Sayles

An Old-Fashioned Girl's Adventures in the Modern World of Dating

An Old-Fashioned Girl's Adventures in the Modern World of Dating

An Old-Fashioned Girl's Adventures in the Modern World of Dating
By April E. Bivens
John McCullough – Editor

Table of Contents

Introduction

This book came about following several restless nights back in 2014. Then it happened. I woke up in the middle of the night and sent a Facebook message to my editor, John, and another friend who is a clinical psychologist, telling them I needed their assistance. I was headed on a book journey. I never had any intention of writing a book, but somehow, someway I was led down that path by no other than our heavenly Father. After several years of dating young, old, rich, broke men, I realized it was time to put my experiences on paper.

Many of my friends always told me, "Your life is like a movie." There are five incredibly memorable dating experiences I will feature in this book. These are five men you may have dated and experiences you can relate to. If you're a man reading this book, welcome! Maybe you can relate to these gentlemen as well. If you fit the profile of one of these men, don't be ashamed! The stories you're about to read are mostly true. I've fictionalized some of the locations and situations, and I changed a few names – mainly to protect the good men I've dated and not embarrass the fools who've entered my life. This book is not intended to bash men. I love men, and while we may be from different universes, we both have one thing in common – the desire to be blessed with a mate who will love us unconditionally. If you're a man reading this, great! I believe this book will enlighten you and help you better communicate with and treat better the women in your life. For everyone, I hope this book makes you laugh, pump your fist, shake your head or help you find a solution to a situation

An Old-Fashioned Girl's Adventures in the Modern World of Dating

you may be going through and perhaps think twice before you step into or out of your next relationship.

An Old-Fashioned Girl's Adventures in the Modern World of Dating

An Old-Fashioned Girl's Adventures in the Modern World of Dating

Chapter 1

Girl Meets Boy

In 2003, I met Michael – the man who would become my son's father, at Shadows nightclub in Atlanta. Yes, we met at "the Club," and I know what you're thinking. I'm not that girl. I've never been the girl who picks up men or who is picked up by men at the Club. I have dated men I met in bookstores, coffee shops, grocery stores, the mall and pretty much everywhere. None of those encounters turned into any great romance, so I figured why not give the guy in the Club a chance. You never know.

I had the pleasure of growing up in a loving two-parent household, with a father who was very protective and who taught me many enduring lessons about dating and relationships. "Never depend on a man for anything," he would say. He taught me values, inspired me with his work ethic, and his love for my mother and my siblings remain the model of the ideal family man.

Sadly, my dad passed away in 2002, just a year before I met Michael.

My girlfriend was in town the night I met Michael. Of course, when a friend comes in town you have to take them to the newest local hot spot, which was club Shadows. She thought Michael was cool. As a matter of fact, she was more excited about him than I was! She definitely thought I needed to exchange phone numbers with him.

An Old-Fashioned Girl's Adventures in the Modern World of Dating

On that fateful night, I wasn't in much of a mood to meet new people, which might explain why I gave Michael the number to my landline – a phone I never answer. I was being polite. I figured he would call me a few times, I'd ignore his calls, and he would get the message. As I suspected, he called on multiple occasions. I finally gave in and called him back. After a week of playing phone tag, we finally spoke. During our first conversation, my cell phone rang. He heard it and said, "I know you did not give me your landline number." I laughed and said, "Yes, I wasn't too sure about you." That phone conversation changed everything. He was a great conversationalist, and from that point forward, our conversations would last for hours.

In the early stages of our dating, Michael and I agreed to meet at club Visions. Yes, Atlanta's famous club Visions that was the hot spot from about 2003-2005!! Michael paid for a VIP booth next to none other than Jay Z. I remember Michael taking charge when I walked up to security to tell them to let me in the VIP section. The security was not admitting anyone because Jay Z had just entered that section with Usher and a few other celebrities. Michael got all up in the security guard's face demanding I be allowed in. He made it clear that he had spent over $5,000 for this section. Two minutes later, I was in!

I loved how aggressive, protective and no-nonsense he could be. It was a turn-on. Jay Z would later walk over to Michael's section and say to him, "I like the way you doing it bro; you are doing it up big tonight." Michael always did everything "Big." We always reminisced about that night, and

An Old-Fashioned Girl's Adventures in the Modern World of Dating

— as we grew more mature — how stupid he was to spend that amount of money. Still, it was a great time; some moments are worth the high price tag.

I guess you could say Michael's and my early days together could classify as a whirlwind romance. After our first two months of dating, he took me to Vegas for the first Jones – Tarver fight. The great time we had in the penthouse at the Venetian hotel was just one of the high points in a relationship that would soon descend to the basement.

Immediately after our Vegas getaway I asked Michael if we were exclusive. He looked me in the eyes and said, "Do you think I would take you to Vegas – first-class all the way – if we were just causally dating?"

Exclusive!

Our first two years of being exclusive were great! We went to some of the best NFL games during the 2004 season. We flew to Philadelphia for a Monday night Eagles-Vikings matchup between Randy Moss, Terrell Owens and Donovan McNabb, with seats on the 50-yard line! We had great seats – no further back than row three – for Alicia Keys, Erykah Badu and Jill Scott...just to name a few.
You could say that I was living every girl's dream – or so I thought until the time came when I wanted that dream to end.

Eight months later I moved in with him into a new house, and the rest was history.

Baby Makes Three

I was deeply in love with Michael. He was a great provider, and I wanted him to be my child's father – so after two years of being together, in 2005 we decided to plan for a baby. I like to plan. I plan everything, right down to the birth of my son. I stopped birth control and met with my doctor, who told me it would take up to a year to get pregnant. I was expecting in six months.

Right about now you might be wondering *if you're such a planner, why didn't you plan to get a ring on your finger before planning to get pregnant?* Perhaps my heart was avoiding the truth that my brain knew all too well. I was ready to be a mom, but not quite ready to be a wife – at least not Michael's.

Michael made sure I was always happy, at least from a material point of view. For my 29th birthday he gave me a four-carat platinum diamond flower ring. A year later it was a Mercedes. Following that, when my son was born, he gave me a Range Rover.

> *Please don't let material goods overshadow or take the place of the truly important things in a relationship like trust, respect and of course quality time.*

I had luxury cars, jewelry and a new roof over my head, but I didn't have the one thing I wanted most – Michael. I talked to my cousin about these feelings, and she said "Girl, stop complaining, you got it made!" I didn't have it made. Michael was very successful and somewhat flashy. Having these two qualities is a recipe for relationship problems, especially in a "small" big city like Atlanta.

The days ahead saw Michael leaving town for work. Fortunately, I had a son to care for, and eventually I grew to care less and less what Michael was doing.

Unfaithful

Two weeks after I returned to work from maternity leave, my sister called, crying hysterically. My first thought was something was wrong with our mother. Despite bracing myself for horrible news, I was still knocked off my feet when my sister said, "Michael is cheating on you with one of my friends!" Staggering, I asked her to repeat herself. The words fell like rocks from the sky...*Michael...cheating.* I rolled with the punch of infidelity, ducked the jab of the reality that Michael was stepping out with someone my sister knew. The knockout blow came later when I ultimately learned Michael had been cheating on me when I was carrying his child.

In a daze, I tried to continue my day. I kept a lunch date with a co-worker, but I wasn't the best company. I didn't eat and just sat there trying to plot my next move. I had too many questions and too few answers. How was I

An Old-Fashioned Girl's Adventures in the Modern World of Dating

going to approach him? Should I wait until he returned home? Oh shit, I needed to call my sister and tell her not to say anything to mom.

Needless to say, that part of my plan came too late, and it wasn't long before mom called to check on me. I did not stay on the phone with her very long. Looking back, I appreciate her reaching out, but in the moment, I was really upset, not at my mom, but because my father wasn't there to help.

My Dad and I were very close. I told him everything. He was the first person I told when I got my period! My Mom and sister were a team, and Dad and I were a team. This was one of those times that I cried out for my Daddy because he would know how to handle this. Heck, he would have given Michael a good piece of his mind.

That evening I called Michael on my way home, he answered, and I immediately said, "So, who the fuck is Lisa? Huh? Huh?" His initial response was a deafening silence. In what felt like minutes later, he finally said, "I don't have time for this right now." "Oh you don't have time," I screamed. "Well the next time you decide to pay her car note, don't forget about the one you have to pay over here." I wasn't finished, "You are fucking my sister's friend, you asshole!! You ought to be thankful my Dad is not alive; he would kick your ass, you dirty dog!" Once again, his response was silence, and with that, I ended the call.

My sister called me back to tell me that the side chick wanted to speak to me, and have a meeting. This really irritated me. What was there to meet about? I had nothing to say. If any meeting were to be scheduled, it would be between Michael and me.

> *I wish I knew why women feel the need to conduct a meeting of the minds to compare notes on the man who is playing them both! This only leads to more hurt and in extreme cases it can set the stage for a nasty physical altercation. The only meeting that should occur is between you and your man. No side chicks allowed!*

I later learned from my sister that Michael had a key to her house and bought new tires for her car – a car whose loan payments he was making!

The one moment of amusement came when my sister told me how the other woman broke out in tears when she learned Michael and I were in a relationship and that two weeks prior Michael was at my sister's house assembling a toy for our son. She became even more unglued when my sister told her that Michael was living with me and that he had given me a new Range Rover.

This young girl – seven years my junior at 24 years of age – had the nerve to cry when the fantasy life she thought she was having turned to dust. All I could do was laugh.

After Michael came home, I forgave him. Yes, I turned the other cheek. After all, I was not looking forward to being a single mother with a 4-month old baby. I wanted to spend my life with him. I thought we could get over this hump. I remember him coming home, and even though he was busted dead to rights, he was still a bit arrogant. "I can leave, just tell me what you want me to do," he said. "I'll pay for everything. I fucked up, and I'm sorry." His apology just didn't seem that sincere.

A week later he bought me two pairs of boots. They were really nice boots, but it didn't matter because I knew they were not a make-up gift. I remember one night looking at his set of keys. There were so many on the ring. I asked him if he gave the key back to the chick. He said he threw it away; I didn't believe him. In that moment I realized that he had thrown us away as well.

I didn't trust him anymore. I stayed for my son. I thought I could forgive and forget — but I couldn't.

I kept wondering: How do women do this? How do they stay after infidelity? Things were never the same.

Even before this life-changing news fell into my lap, Michael and I had begun living separate lives. The official end – if you want to call it that – would come shortly after New Year's Day 2009. Michael was traveling, and I asked him when he would be home. He said he wasn't sure. Maybe that was the push I needed for me to tell him finally I was finished. I was

An Old-Fashioned Girl's Adventures in the Modern World of Dating

unhappy and I couldn't do this anymore. He thought I was joking, but the cry in my voice was clear indication that I was serious. His response was to turn the tables and accuse me of cheating on him.

He finally returned home a week later. Sadly, he acted as if we had never spoken about my desire to end the relationship. Face to face, I told him again I was done. He couldn't look me in my eyes – eyes that were free of tears. What started as a penthouse fantasy ended on the ground floor of reality. My heavy heart was ready to beat again.

After the break up, I finally felt a sense of relief. This heavy burden lifted, I felt lighter and was able to breathe again.

Was I sad and hurt when it ended? Yes! I wanted a family, and I thought we would spend our lives together. There was no denying how much he loved me, and I loved him. We had so much in common, so many good times but I knew deep down that I was not meant to be with a man I could not trust.

I regret that it took so long for me to let go. We all have to do things on our own time. I had just had a baby when I found out. Who knows, I may have been going through postpartum depression. Maybe that's why I could not leave. Maybe I wanted to hold on to the hope that one day I would fully trust him again, but it didn't happen.

An Old-Fashioned Girl's Adventures in the Modern World of Dating

Seven years later, he is married to a nice woman who has always been loving toward my son. That's all you can hope for when you part ways after having a child — the person your ex ends up with will show love and compassion for your child. As I write these memories, Michael recently shared with me that when people ask what happened between us, he makes sure to tell them that he fucked up our relationship. A large part of that is because he wasn't ready.

After more than five years of being the loyal, submissive woman — who gave so much to a relationship only to receive so little (beyond the material) in return — I was ready to love again and eventually trust again. It was time to write a new chapter. With nothing but my intuition and my eyes wide open, this 34-year-old single mom was ready to find a new happily ever after.

Chapter 2

Broken Bones and Broken Dreams

It was April 2011, and I had taken a break from dating. I was focused on getting my son ready for kindergarten in the fall. I was so over the Atlanta dating scene, or so I thought. My hair stylist at the time was a married woman who was always telling me stories about her single friends. One day during my appointment, she mentioned that one of her friends was getting really serious with a guy she met online. My stylist then asked, "Have you ever tried online dating?" Laughing, I said no. She recommended a particular dating site and told me I should try it. Her belief was that all the people on dating sites are looking to settle down and enter exclusive relationships. I decided to take her advice and give it a try. Heck, I'm a big believer in trying new things, and who knows? I might just get lucky enough to meet the man of my dreams.

I created my profile and it was on! I was getting more than 20 hits a day! I wasn't interested in all 20 of those prospects, but at least three each day piqued my interest. I would chat back and forth with these men for at least a week before I would be comfortable enough to give them my number. Usually, all I needed was a phone conversation to decipher if I wanted to continue communicating with someone. I would meet some guys at coffee shops or for lunch during the workweek. I made it a point to send my friends pictures and the profiles of the men I was meeting – for security purposes – and for girl talk later.

An Old-Fashioned Girl's Adventures in the Modern World of Dating

There was this one man who made it through my screening process. His name was David. He contacted me, but I didn't respond right away. I showed my friend the picture and profile and she said, "Ohhhh he is handsome, good career, contact him. What are you waiting on?" I wasn't sure why I was reluctant to contact him. At the time, there was something about him I just couldn't figure out. It was his picture. Something about that photo triggered my instincts. In retrospect, it was another time in my dating life when there were red flags begging me to stop.

I responded to David's message and we started chatting on the phone. The phone conversation went well, and I was open to meeting him for a drink. We

O.K., here is the deal. We all see red flags early on in the dating process. We just tend to ignore them and let certain things slide because we want that person to be the one. Now in my 40s, I'm smart enough to know when the red flag is flying that it's time to run.

decided to meet at a restaurant that has these frozen margaritas I love. I know my limit, especially on a first date. I get flirtatious when I drink so I made sure just to have one margarita. I arrived at the restaurant about 10 minutes before him. I was anxiously waiting outside when he pulled up. I hate when a man is late on the first date. As he was walking toward me a voice in my head said, "Damn he is fine, this dating website is great."

An Old-Fashioned Girl's Adventures in the Modern World of Dating

David was on the phone with his mom when he approached me. He spoke very kindly to her, which really impressed me.

I was nervous as we walked into the restaurant. I hate the official first date; it is nothing more than an interview in casual clothing. We were having fun, as we nibbled on appetizers. My drink was great and so was he until David made a comment that should have been an indicator of his immaturity. Once again, I ignored a sign.

David asked me how old I was, claiming he couldn't remember from my profile. He damn near dropped his drink when I told him I was 36. Laughing, I modestly said, "Yes, I know I look 28. I have my grandmother's good genes!" He too laughed as he responded, "Yes, I thought you were 27 or 28. I usually don't date women your age." At this point, in my mind I'm playing back our earlier conversations. I recall David mentioning he was 35, which made me believe we were the same age. Snapping back to reality, I asked, "Why don't you date women my age?" His answer hit harder than the tequila in my cocktail. "You all are too set in your ways," said David. "You think you are so grown and act like you are 50."

An Old-Fashioned Girl's Adventures in the Modern World of Dating

If that weren't bad enough, he continued, "Younger women are more outgoing and spontaneous!"

Who the hell did this man think he was fooling? Please allow me to translate. What David wanted to say was that younger women are easy. Younger women aren't really worried about commitments and marriage. They go with the flow. They can be manipulated. Call them at midnight (Two hours past my bedtime, thank you!) and they'll be in your bed by 1:00!

This was more than a red flag. It was like a fire alarm blaring in my head. Yet, I ignored it because we had a connection. Once again, you live and you learn.

Despite David's dissertation on the virtues of dating younger women, we still had a great time, and I couldn't wait for our second date. When I got home, I was all smiles. My sister was babysitting, and she met me at the door when I got home. Before I could walk in, she said, "Wow, this online dating is working for you!" At the time, I had to agree.

Over the next three days, David and I exchanged texts. We had a phone conversation where we discussed seeing each other over the upcoming weekend. Saturday finally came. I was anxiously looking forward to seeing

An Old-Fashioned Girl's Adventures in the Modern World of Dating

him again, when I received a text. I couldn't believe what I was reading on my phone. David was in the hospital with a broken leg. He had fallen off a ladder while doing some work around the house. He was totally immobile and according to his doctors, he was lucky to be alive.

I was thankful to hear he was O.K., yet I was still in shock. David said he would be in the hospital for a few more days. I asked him if he wanted company during his hospital stay. He waved me off, saying he would rather wait to see me when he returned home. Later I would find out that he had all the company he needed courtesy of a woman he used to date who flew into town to hold his hand at his bedside.

He was finally released from the hospital and back at home. For the first two days, he had the assistance of a private nurse. David had screws in his leg and was looking at a total of nine months of recovery and physical therapy. He was on pain meds, so we only spoke on the phone. A week had gone by before he asked me to stop by his house one evening after work.

After he gave me his address, I couldn't believe we lived just eight minutes away from each other. I arrived at his house and his mother answered the door. After she looked me up and down – as only a man's mother can do – she smiled and welcomed me in.

An Old-Fashioned Girl's Adventures in the Modern World of Dating

David was on a recliner in the basement. His face lit up, and he smiled as I entered the room. Despite the sight of David in a barbaric leg brace and the obvious pain he was enduring, I still managed to return his smile.

He looked at me and said, "I wasn't expecting our second date to be like this." He looked so uncomfortable so I asked him if he needed anything. He asked me to move his pillow, and I did. We were close when I moved his pillow and my sudden rapid heartbeat was evidence of how much I was really attracted to him. It was getting late, and he looked as if he needed some rest. His mother escorted me out of the basement, and we spoke briefly. She looked tired. I told her if she needed a break to let me know. I was willing to be David's nurse while she got some much-needed rest.

Things moved quickly between David and me. I would frequently stop at his house before I picked up my son from summer camp. His mother and I became more and more friendly, and she made it clear to me that there were other women stopping by to see him but none like me (Yeah, I know – another red flag!). Then one day, she came out and said, "I like you. I want him to pick you because you have done the most out of all of them." I always knew that dating was a competition but she was just reconfirming what I already knew.

David and his Mother kept asking me to stop by with my son. I was very uneasy about that, even though she was a retired elementary teacher and was once a single mother herself. I still did not want to introduce my son

An Old-Fashioned Girl's Adventures in the Modern World of Dating

to anyone I was not seriously considering for an exclusive relationship. His mom would say, "April he can stay up here with me while you visit with David," she continued. "You need to see how David and your son interact, just introduce him as your friend. You and my son are friends, right?" I finally gave in and introduced my son to David and his mother. I was nervous, but everything went well. I finally started feeling like this could be the man with whom I enter into an exclusive relationship.

He was confined to the recliner for about three weeks. I would bring him food, massage his leg, help him to the restroom, help him shave and bathe. I was David's makeshift nurse throughout his entire recovery, nurturing this man back to good health like he was my husband and had been for years. I took him out in the wheelchair. Yes, I was rolling around the ATL with a wheelchair in the trunk of my car.

David finally said to me, "April you know I was dating about three women when I first met you. I even had an out of town ex come back to visit, but she didn't stay long because she was getting upset that female friends were visiting me." He mentioned he and this ex got into an argument, which led to his mother all but bouncing her out of the hospital room. After sharing this revelation, he told me that I had succeeded in knocking those other women off the list. He didn't say the words, but it was pretty clear that we were becoming exclusive. I tried to see him every day, and if I couldn't, he would tell me how much he missed me.

An Old-Fashioned Girl's Adventures in the Modern World of Dating

I was finally falling in love again. Sadly, all good things do come to an end. For me, that end snuck up on me. His mother decided to leave because she felt that he was in good hands with me. She told him to treat me right, and before she left she whispered in my ear, "I hope you are the one he marries, I love you!" With his mother gone, and with David inching closer to a full recovery, I began to see a change.

I took a day off from work to take him to the orthopedist. He was having an in-patient surgical procedure to have pins removed from his leg. After I had scheduled a sick day, he kept saying he didn't need me to take him to the doctor. This led me to wonder if someone else was taking him. Was there some other woman? I did wind up taking him to the doctor. David left his phone with me while he was undergoing the procedure. The phone rang several times, but I didn't look to see who it was. I've never been one to check my man's cell phone or emails and I wasn't about to start now.

It's funny how the little things can suddenly turn into a big pile of problems. Such was the case between David and me. When I remarked to David that my son, who always opened the door for me, was more of a gentleman than he was, he got angry. When David saw a pair of old rims my son's father was innocently storing in my garage, he got jealous. One time, after he returned to Atlanta after an unannounced trip out of town, he went to a concert with a woman who gave him tickets. After the show, he wanted to come by and have an encore with me. I'm not saying I was perfect, but while David was recovering from his injuries, I really bent over backward to help him. But once he got back on his feet, he changed.

An Old-Fashioned Girl's Adventures in the Modern World of Dating

He was becoming less and less the man I thought I was falling in love with.

After a pretty heated argument where I got everything off my chest, I finally found the courage to break it off with him. It was during the fall, but by the following winter he was calling and texting me non-stop. He wanted to see me, but I ignored his calls and texts. This went on for two months until I finally decided to see him.

We met at a local coffee shop. I began to feel agitated as I saw him through the window. He was waiting for me at a table. By the time I got inside and sat down, I looked at him and felt no attraction. B.B. King was singing in my head… the thrill is gone!! As I approached his table I began to wonder what the hell was I thinking! He's not even that cute anymore. I've been told when I'm done with someone I have this look in my eyes that screams "I don't give a fuck what you're saying!" That look was in full beast mode that day.

He was all smiles and seemed somewhat nervous as I arrived at the table. His smile dimmed when I told him I had plans later that evening and I only had 30 minutes to spare. David got off to a good start when he said how much he missed me, but he fell off the ladder again when he went on about how I needed to learn that he is the type of man who comes and goes as he pleases. Twenty-five minutes to go. He went on to say that he doesn't want the responsibility of checking in with me regarding his whereabouts. He said I acted like his probation officer. I laughed so hard everyone turned around and glanced at us. I guess David was feeling pretty good about himself. After all of the calls and texts and pleading to meet with me, this is the best he could come up with? Fifteen minutes to go. Suppressing the urge to laugh squarely in his face, I tightened my jaw and said, "David you obviously don't understand the importance of respect and communication in a relationship." My blood pressure rising, I continued. "I don't give a damn where you go, but it you don't have enough respect to say 'Hey April, I'm heading out of town for a few days,' then we are both wasting our time." And speaking of time, David's 30 minutes were up.

Regaining my composure, I politely told him I needed to go home to get ready for a date. He laughed and said, "Cancel it!" I laughed harder and said, "You are crazy!" I guess his broken limbs were fully healed, because he had no trouble following me as I made like Usain Bolt and damn near sprinted to my car. I got to my car and as I closed the door, David made his Hail Mary move and leaned forward to try to kiss me. I turned my face away, and his pass was incomplete. He asked, "Don't you love me?" I answered "No," and drove off.

Before I could pull into my garage he was texting me saying how good it was to see me and how much he missed and loved me and could we see each other tomorrow. Feeling a sense of calm, I replied to his text with this very simple message: "David, we are obviously in two different places. I need to be with someone who is respectful and interested in communicating with me; you have a lot of growing to do. I wish you all

An Old-Fashioned Girl's Adventures in the Modern World of Dating

the best in life." Seconds later, he responded with, "O.K, April I love you."

Two weeks later he began texting again. This time every other day. The texts were accompanied by emails saying he loved me. His calls and texts went unanswered and he continued trying to get my attention for nearly the first half of 2012, from February through July. On average, I would receive at least four texts a month during this timeframe. By the time 2012 arrived, I wasn't seriously dating anyone. Of course David was still texting me, but one particular text caught me by surprise. It was more than the regular, "I love you text." This one had some substance to it. "Hi April, how are you? I really miss you. I want to talk to you about some things and I have something for you." Hmmmm, now he's trying to get to me with gifts. I responded and told him to put it in the mail. David texted back saying that he realized our last encounter was a failure and he wanted another chance to make things right. The begging was beginning to wear on me, plus I was kind of bored and in need of a little comedic relief. So I agreed (again) to meet him.

Even though he suggested one of my favorite restaurants, I suggested another location. I didn't want him controlling the situation. I arrived at the restaurant first, which provided me the opportunity to see him as he came into the dining room. I heard that voice in my head again saying, "What the hell is going on?" Any attraction I had from our very first meeting had long disappeared. David arrived with a gift bag in his hand. The hostess showed us to our table, and we sat down. He was better prepared this time. The words rolled off of his tongue, and I damn near fell out of my chair. "April I want to apologize for the way I treated you. I had a lot going on and I was not fair to you. You played a major role in my recovery and if it wasn't for you I don't know if I would be walking right now."

Well I'll be damned!! This man finally woke the hell up, but it was too damn late! He even went further and asked me to give him another chance. He wanted to start dating again. I felt a drop of compassion when he mentioned that his mother had been asking about me. He told the story of how he and his mother smiled and thought about me while shopping at the mall and smelling the distinctive scent of my favorite perfume. Then he handed me the gift bag, which contained a bottle of my favorite fragrance. I had to admit, I was shocked. David brought his "A" game, and he was sincere. I decided to give him another chance. They say the third time is a charm. Let's hope 'they' are right!

I was intensely determined to control the pace of our relationship. I'm not the type of woman to go to a man's house on the second date, but due to the unique circumstances surrounding his accident and injuries, I guess I let my guard down the first time around. This time I made sure things would be different.

We started dating again. We went to a jazz spot, and we had a nice time. David picked me up and since this was technically our second date since getting back together, he assumed I would ask him in. Bad assumption! I looked him in the eyes and thanked him for a nice time. He laughed and

An Old-Fashioned Girl's Adventures in the Modern World of Dating

said, "O.K., I get it." This routine would go on for about six more dates. One time, he went as far as to get out of the car and follow me up the steps to my home. As he trailed behind me, I turned and told him he was not coming in until I felt comfortable with where our relationship was heading. He walked away so sad, shaking his head. This was great! I was in control, and loving it. I was running this on my terms.

One day David called me and asked if he could take me to the mall with him. I agreed. When we arrived at the mall, I got out of the car. I shook my head. He asked what was wrong. I told him that it bothered me that he refused to open the car door for me, and to top it off, my six-year-old son is mannerly enough to open the door for a lady. Irritated, he looked at me and said he doesn't open car doors for me, his mother or any other woman. Once again the inner voice started talking in my head, "What are you doing wasting your time with this immature man child?," which was ironically followed with David telling me that I should probably be dating older men because they do stuff like opening car doors. We still went into the mall, but this was pretty much the end of the conversation. As we were walking in the mall I showed him something, and he just ignored me. I asked him what was wrong. He turned and said, "You know what I don't feel like this; let's go." Things went downhill from here.

As we walked out of the mall, David suddenly turned into a man of rage. He began to mumble. I told him I couldn't hear what he was saying. Looking back, I wish I hadn't asked him to repeat himself. He snapped, "You get on my damn nerves! Who the fuck do you think you are?"

An Old-Fashioned Girl's Adventures in the Modern World of Dating

Stunned, I wondered what was causing this rage. I asked him what was his problem. I got no answer; he just told me to get in the car. I thought for a moment that I should take a cab home because he was beginning to look crazy — not in a cute "you so crazy" way, but downright nuts! Still, I got in the car. We didn't say anything to each other, but then all of a sudden David went off! "Who the hell do you think you are some queen?" he said. (In my mind, I like to think I am!) "You ain't shit! You make me sick. I don't give a damn about a car door! I'm not that dude. Who the hell have you been dating?" His verbal explosion continued with his screaming, "Fuck you and opening up a car door! How dare you compare me to your son! Fuck you." I looked, laughed and said, "You are crazy! Something is wrong with you!" He responded, "Yeah! You, that's what's wrong with me. I've taken you out seven, eight times, and you think you're all that! You won't let me in your house! Fuck you." This time, I obeyed my instincts, and as a result David was mad because I wasn't rushing him into my bedroom.

We were about five minutes from my house and he was driving recklessly. I was in deep prayer when I noticed that he missed the turn to my neighborhood. Instead, out of nowhere, he asked me if I liked a particular restaurant on the other side of the highway. I began to wonder if falling off the ladder also rendered David bipolar! I was in no mood to spend any more time with this man. I screamed, "Take me home now! I don't want to spend another minute in your presence." He had fury in his eyes, and I continued to pray. I sat silently while he cursed at me as he sped down the street. We finally pulled into my subdivision. He was still yelling. I don't

An Old-Fashioned Girl's Adventures in the Modern World of Dating

remember much of what he said, except his parting words, which remain burned in my memory. "Good luck finding you a pristine ass nigga!! Fuck you bitch, I'm done." I hopped out of that car and didn't look back.

Now at 41, would I do it all over again for another man who I just started dating, as I did for David? Probably not. What's sad about that is men and women have to realize that their actions can lead to hurt, which can in turn affect the next relationship of the person who you treated so badly. We build up walls due to previous experiences. We could potentially miss out on a great person because of these walls. I guess we all have to be open to possibly getting hurt again or possibly encountering love again. We always bounce back, as I did. I just need to be more patient and not dive in too quickly.

Update: To this day, I wonder what he was "done" with. It certainly wasn't any vestige of a relationship. During my second round with David, he wanted to take control, but I made sure to retain the upper hand. I really couldn't care less what issues were going through his sick mind.

Shortly after writing this chapter on David, I ran into him at the Atlanta airport. At first glance, I was not sure it was him, until he walked closer. I could feel him looking at me through the dark shades he was wearing. I turned my head, he walked right past me, and neither of us spoke. Within minutes I had an email from him professing his love, and revealing how he still wanted to be with me, and that one day soon he wanted to be my husband. He commented how he could not get my signature scent out of his mind as he had just seen/smelled me. I never responded, but I did read the email a couple of times. I wondered why he didn't speak but took the time to write an email. I guess he was scared or maybe he could see the disgust in my eyes as he passed me. One thing I do know is that this was just more confirmation my story about him was meant to be shared in these pages.

In another twist of irony, it was David's mother who told me that God is going to bless me with an amazing man. I think we both knew that David was not going to be that man.

Thank you David for being another chapter in my life, and this book.

Chapter 3

Fumble on the Play

When I was 12, my father moved our family from upstate New York to New Orleans to expose us to a little more diversity. After the first year in New Orleans, he made sure to tell me that New Orleans was a great place to live, but he felt there were more professional opportunities for me outside of New Orleans. I contemplated moving to California, back to New York or to Atlanta. It took just one visit to the black mecca of the South, and within 30 days I was packed and ready to start my new life in Atlanta.

The year was 2000, I was 25 years old and getting settled in Atlanta, but when Labor Day rolled around, I was looking forward to spending that holiday weekend in Miami. I called a friend who lived there and asked her if I could stay with her over Labor Day weekend. She said yes! Miami was the place to be Labor Day weekend. Everyone had descended on South Beach — athletes, rappers and the who's who from most every city around the U.S.

On my last night in Miami, we went to this club – a real hot spot. I remember exactly what I wore. It was a cat suit! Yes, at 25 I was wearing a cat suit and I was wearing it well! This baby blue skintight ensemble was turning heads. As my friend and I walked out of the club, I was stopped by a famous point guard for the Houston Rockets. He was cute, but I've never been one to date an athlete, although flirting wasn't out of the question, which we did until my friend looked at me and pointed to her

An Old-Fashioned Girl's Adventures in the Modern World of Dating

watch. It was 4 a.m. and time to go. My friend was 20 years old and still lived in her parent's house, and sometimes her parents would get on her about coming in late.

As we walked to the valet, we turned when we heard a group of mopeds whiz by. The men on the bikes were well built, and they looked so handsome zipping through South Beach. One of the men sped by and quickly turned around. He slowly eased up next to me, and all I could see were his hazel eyes. Damn this guy was fine. He removed his helmet and my jaw dropped as I saw a man who could pass for a more handsome version of L.L. Cool J. He wore a white t-shirt that not only complemented his impressive physique, but it provided a nice contrast to his caramel skin. Add this to those hazel eyes and his boyish dimples and I was immediately mesmerized. He said hello and asked my name. I smiled and said, "April and who are you?" He said his name was James. As soon as he started speaking, I was in love. He told me he was from California.

I exchanged numbers with James, just before he mounted his bike and sped off. Meeting James was the perfect ending to my last night in Miami. Not long after I returned to Atlanta, James called me. He was still in Miami, we chatted a few times, and we enjoyed great conversations. James was a 30-year-old real estate agent and artist manager. Previously, he was an R&B artist. He proved to be more than just a pretty face. He was very articulate, wrote poetry and had a witty sense of humor. I was intrigued. He asked me how I felt about dating someone out of state, and I told him I was open to it. We spent about two weeks chatting on the phone before he came to Atlanta to see me. We had a great time. When he accompanied

An Old-Fashioned Girl's Adventures in the Modern World of Dating

me to a wedding, people kept asking us if we were brother and sister. We shared the same complexion and eye color, which was a fact that did not go unnoticed by James. He would always comment on how pretty our children would be.

As we got to know each other I found out he was Muslim. This was the first time I had ever dated a Muslim man. It was interesting to see him follow his faith's ritual of prayer several times during the day. James didn't drink alcohol and was a pescatarian. I have no problem dating a pescatarian, but please don't give me a thesis on why I should not eat meat or any of the virtues of eating clean. He was also a fitness buff. He gave me exercise DVDS, and he motivated me to go to the gym five days a week. In hindsight, I would say James had a tendency to be controlling.

We became exclusive after a month, and we saw each other every two weeks. He'd either fly me to California or he would come to Atlanta. One of our visits lasted two weeks. We got along pretty well, but it didn't take long to see that there were some things we didn't have in common. One glaring example was football. From the time I was six years old, I spent Sunday afternoons watching football with my father. Sunday game day was very special to me, and unfortunately this is where James and I clashed. One particular Sunday, I was visiting James in California. I was ready to lie around and watch football all day. He wasn't. It was almost time for kickoff, when he said, "Let's get ready." I didn't know what he was getting ready for. I wanted to watch the games and had no plans of leaving the house. He gave me a confused look and said, "Come on, why do you even watch football? What's the point?" He continued, "You're here to see me. Are they paying you to watch the game?" At that point, I not only heard that inner voice telling me this wasn't going to work, I saw it standing at the 50-yard line in a striped ref's jersey tossing a yellow penalty flag! My previous boyfriends were big football fans, and I couldn't believe I was arguing with a man about wanting to watch a game. He then stormed out of the room. He spent the rest of the day texting on his 2-way pager, and I couldn't care less. I was enjoying my football.

During this same visit we went to a concert to see one of the artists he managed. Just before we left the house, he looked me up and down and proclaimed my jeans were too tight and my sweater was too low cut. He ordered me to change. I was beginning to see more and more controlling aspects of him, which I did not like. I didn't think I was dressing too suggestively, but James said his religion dictated that I dress more conservatively. I respected that, but I still thought this was another example of his controlling personality. I saw myself beginning to change for him – more than just clothes – and I didn't like it. I was 25 and had one daddy, and I wasn't looking for another one.

New Year's Eve rolled around, and I traveled to California to ring in the New Year with James. We argued the entire trip. He was on the phone constantly with his female best friend, which left me feeling disrespected. As we were leaving to go to his friend's house, he stopped to look at me and said, "I don't think we're going to work out. We're too different, and you seem somewhat needy." He then casually said, "Let's go to this party and act as if were still together." He didn't want to have to explain this sudden break-up to his friends. I was glad our brief four-month relationship was over, but the idea of role-playing seemed quite childish. Still, I went along with the plan. We went to the party, and all his friends were so happy to see us. Some of them asked me when I was going to move to California. Never being one to hide my feelings, anyone could clearly see that I was aggravated the entire evening. His friends asked me what was wrong, and I simply responded that I had a headache. We left the party at midnight, and instead of wishing me a Happy New Year, he chastised my poor attitude. With obvious frustration in my voice, I reminded him that he had broken up with me, and the Brad and Angelina act we just put on for his friends disgusted me. Looking back, this was not one of my happiest New Year's Eve celebrations.

We returned to his place, and I immediately tried to change my flight to the next morning. The weather was horrible, and it grounded all California departures. As I contemplated my next move, I overheard him on the phone telling someone about our abrupt break-up. The words that were the loudest were the ones that stung the most – "I just couldn't take her anymore…" Soon after James hung up he let me know that he was in love with his best friend and that was another reason why we were breaking up.

> *It's been said that one should marry their best friend. Ladies, this is why you must keep your guard up when you meet a man whose 'best friend' is a woman other than yourself!*

This was all I could take. I screamed, "How dare you have me come to California just to break up with me on New Year's Eve, and then tell me about your new love!" Tears followed my screams, and my crying was soon followed by hyperventilating. It had become hard to breathe. I regained some of my composure and managed to call my mother to tell her what happened. She connected my sister on a three-way call, and together they tried to calm me down. James heard me on the phone. He came over, and he too tried to calm me down. It took two days, but I finally escaped from California. I've since learned there are few things worse than being stranded, due to bad weather, away from home, especially when you're with someone who has just broken up with you.

It was a new year and I spent the first month of it in a funk, thanks to James. I eventually met someone else who wiped away any memories of James, and my life went on. Fast forward eight years to 2009, and guess who tried to re-enter my life? You got it: James.

In 2009, the year I ended things with my son's father, I set up a Facebook page. Within two months, I received a friend request from James. This immediately triggered horrible memories. It would be a month before I would accept his friend request. I was curious to see what he had been up to and why he was trying to contact me.

We did chat on the phone, and he apologized for how terribly he handled our relationship. He said he was a boy then, and was a man now. He told me he and his *best friend* did not work out and he regretted ever letting me go, but he was too young to see it then. He asked about my relationship status, and I told him I had been dating for the past eight months. James was living in Houston and wanted to know if he could fly me down to see if we could rekindle what we had. I was certainly not expecting that! Things had changed. I was no longer a 25-year-old girl with a crush. I was now a 34-year-old with a son, but his persistence outweighed my reluctance. After all, he apologized so many times I began to think that maybe he was truly interested in another chance. I decided to see if we could first be friends before even considering anything beyond that. It was October, and by December I was heading to Houston.

In an unplanned case of irony, I would again be spending time with James during football season. The New Orleans Saints were 13 and 0 and were set to play the Dallas Cowboys. Any diehard fan will remember that game. James booked my ticket to Houston on the same Saturday the game was scheduled. I glanced at my itinerary and screamed when I saw the time. My flight was departing at 4 p.m. and arriving in Houston at 5:30 p.m. Kickoff for the Saints game was at 4:15 p.m. By the time my flight landed, and I could make my way to a television, I was certain to miss the first half of the game. I admit it was my idea to leave on Saturday and return Monday morning. This was the first time I had seen him since the breakup in 2001, and I wanted to make sure I did not get stuck again. I called James to tell him we had a problem with the time of my flight to Houston and I asked if it could be moved to an earlier departure. He told me he had a few meetings Saturday morning and the afternoon was the best time for me to arrive. I told him how serious this game was, and he was very accommodating, even going as far to tell me about a sports bar we could go to that was only 15 minutes from the airport. I reluctantly agreed to leave Atlanta as scheduled. To my surprise, James had now

An Old-Fashioned Girl's Adventures in the Modern World of Dating

become a football fan. He made plans for us to go to a sports bar on Sunday so I could watch football all day. I don't know what changed over the past nine years, but he was now interested in the game. He even mentioned that his Raiders and Chargers were playing and he needed to see them both win. I didn't tell him that hometown pride was one thing, but pick a side already!

My flight was on time. As soon as I got off the plane, I turned my phone on with the intention of checking the Saints-Cowboys score, but instead I saw that James had anxiously called to let me know he was waiting for me in the passenger waiting area. That was nice, but I was more concerned with checking the score. I keyed in ESPN in my cell phone browser and to my disbelief the Saints were losing. I needed to get to a television ASAP! I wanted to turn around and go home because it was my fault New Orleans was getting beat. I should have been watching the game from the first play, and this might be why I barely smiled when I saw James in the passenger waiting area. He asked what was wrong, and all I could say was "The Saints are losing. Get me to a TV ASAP!" We jumped in his car, and he drove like a bandit. I almost forgot about the game, when I saw his speedometer hit 100 mph. We arrived at the sports bar in one piece. By the way, it wasn't a true sports bar, just a restaurant with a bunch of TVs. At this point, I was too excited to nitpick. As the final plays flashed across the screen, he kept trying to engage in conversation. I briefly glanced away from the action to let him know that it was important I focus on the game. We would talk after the Saints win, but that didn't happen. The Cowboys beat my beloved Saints. It was the first loss of the season and it made me feel miserable. My head and my stomach ached! James told me

An Old-Fashioned Girl's Adventures in the Modern World of Dating

he was sorry and I wanted to tell him to go fuck himself because this devastating loss was his fault! My phone was exploding with commiserating calls and texts from those who loved the Saints and gloating messages from those who didn't. All of my friends and family knew I bled New Orleans black and gold. I spent several minutes on the phone before we left the restaurant. I was not in the mood to talk (or do much else) with James. Any chances for a pleasant weekend went out the window with the dashed hopes of an undefeated Saints season.

We arrived at James' place and the first thing I saw were a dozen white roses waiting for me on his kitchen counter. He was really trying hard. I was still in a pissy mood, yet I tried to force a smile. Calls and texts about the game were still lighting up my phone. Clearly aggravated, James finally said, "When are you going to put your phone down?" I looked at him, rolled my eyes and sneered this was the first loss of the season, and I'll put the phone away when I'm done.

The game and the loss wore me out and I was ready for a good night's sleep. I think James had something else in mind. I wrapped up my hair and put on my night clothes – nothing fancy, just a pair of boy shorts and a tank top. James kept telling me how happy he was to see me, but all I wanted was to go to sleep. The next morning, I woke up to find James' hands around me. I retreated to my side of the bed. This was not the time for romance. I needed to know if he had changed and if we could be friends again. James slowly awoke, smiled, and asked me if I felt better about the Saints loss. I told him that it still hurt. This encouraged him to slide closer to me and ask if he could make the pain feel better. With more

An Old-Fashioned Girl's Adventures in the Modern World of Dating

urgency in my voice, I said no. Ignoring me, James advanced again, and again I said no. Then he outright grabbed me. Time had stopped as I came to grips with the fact I was now fighting to get this 225-pound man off me. As I struggled, he told me to relax. He said, "You know we used to have great sex, just relax." Fight or flight kicked in. Since flight wasn't working, I decided to fight. I started throwing lefts and rights, but it wasn't until I screamed "get the fuck off of me, you're scaring me…" did he accept that I was serious – no meant no. He backed off, and I ran into the bathroom and closed the door. He came to the door and began to apologize and beg me to come out. I managed to grab my phone when I ran into the bathroom. I used it to text the handful of people I knew in California. One person I knew would be willing to help was out of town, but she told me I could call her brother if things got worse. I finally exited the bathroom and it looked as if James had been crying. He pleaded with me and admitted he had crossed the line and got carried away. He said all he wanted was for things to be better between us. James' attempt to have sex with me was proof that things were moving way too quickly. I told him it would be best for him to take me to a hotel. Again he apologized and he agreed to give me some space. He got the message and I knew he wouldn't touch me again without my permission. I eventually agreed to stay with him at his place.

Later that same day, he took me to a sports bar to watch football. It bothered me that he was now a football fan. Where did this come from? He couldn't stand football nine years ago, now he roots for two teams (in the same market, which to this day I find comical). I stopped questioning why James was now Mr. Football. It was flattering that he took a strong interest in something he knew I liked. For once I began to relax and enjoy what turned out to be a nice Sunday afternoon. I watched all the football I wanted and was finally getting over the Saints loss. It was close to 7 p.m. by the time we left the sports bar.

He said he wanted to cook for me and I remembered what a good cook he was. We picked up a few groceries and returned to his place. He prepared an amazing dinner. Things had improved from the previous evening, but it was clear that I wasn't as attracted to him as I was that night we first met outside the club in South Beach. It's funny how one's likes and dislikes can change over the span of nine years.

Monday morning finally arrived and I was ready to go home. I thanked him for the weekend. He responded with another apology for acting so aggressively in the bedroom. In an attempt to end things on a positive note, he told me how glad he was that we reconnected and he hoped he'd get to see me again. James seemed sincere, but I just didn't have the same feelings for him. As soon as I landed in Atlanta, I went straight to work, which helped take my mind off the events of the previous weekend. Later that afternoon, James sent me a message via Facebook. Again, he apologized. He also said how good it was we reconnected. He hoped I could see that I still have a place in his heart. I responded with a simple 'thank you.' The weekend visit was a mistake. I didn't want to see him again. The next day he emailed a poem he wrote for me. It was beautiful, but it was a rhyme intended for the 25-year-old girl I was, not the 34-year-old woman I had become.

An Old-Fashioned Girl's Adventures in the Modern World of Dating

My curiosity was satisfied. I closed the chapter on James, or so I thought, until January 2012, when he reentered my life.

It was more than a year before James reached out to me. He was still apologizing for the Houston incident, and I could tell how sincere he was. I started to think maybe I should give him just one more chance. Looking back, there were a lot of variables that contributed to the horrible weekend, the Saints loss being the major one. We chatted a few times on the phone. He told me that he had moved to Baltimore, which happened to be close to where my mom lived. He asked me if I was in an exclusive relationship. Since I wasn't, he suggested we should try a do-over. He offered to fly me to Baltimore so we could see each other under better circumstances. I reluctantly agreed, and I was happy to hear that he would not book my ticket until after the football season.

He booked my ticket for a Friday afternoon arrival and a Sunday afternoon departure. I told him my mother lived 45 minutes away from him and that I wanted to surprise her on Saturday afternoon. He had no problems with my plan. He said it was ironic that she lived so close to him. I arrived on Friday around 2 p.m. with an empty stomach, and I was starving. I had caught a noon flight with no time to grab lunch.

James was waiting for me upon my arrival. He walked me to his car, and no sooner than I got in the vehicle, he told me he had to run some errands before we got on the road to Atlantic City. Atlantic City? I just landed, and now we were going to drive three hours to a place I really did not feel like going? Oh boy here we go! I was not getting a good feeling about this. His errands included stops at the bank, the cleaners, the gas station, the car wash and the grocery store! What the heck was going on? What kind of guy –

> **Guys, if you want to stay on your lady's good side, and avoid the rage that accompanies an empty stomach, make sure to ask, "Honey, are you hungry?", and please don't get between her and a good meal.**

who's trying to mend a relationship – invites a woman for the weekend and spends the entire afternoon running errands? He claimed he had been so busy and this was the only time he had to get everything done. It was now 5 p.m. and my hunger pangs quickly migrated north and left me with a splitting headache. He said we had to go to his house, pack and then we would head to Atlantic City for dinner. I told him I was starving and suggested we have dinner first. Thankfully, he agreed.

Dinner was nice, and I was feeling better now that I finally had some food in my system. It was after 7:30 p.m. by the time we finished dinner, and my cousin called asking if we could meet her in downtown Silver Spring. I told James that we could just hang out in Maryland instead of driving to Atlantic City, but he was fixated on this trip.

An Old-Fashioned Girl's Adventures in the Modern World of Dating

It was 9:30 p.m. by the time we left for Atlantic City. I had been up since 6 that morning, and the more tired I became, the more my aggravation grew.

On the road to Atlantic City James spent most of the ride on the phone discussing work. He was talking incredibly loudly and he repeatedly said to me, "This is work, hold on, I'm sorry, I'm just so busy!" Even off the phone, he wanted to talk about work. Sensing my irritation, he finally decided to ask about me and my son 'Mike.' Mike? Who the hell was Mike? "Who are you talking about?" I said. "My son's name is not Mike." He then offered a weak apology and said he was thinking about an employee named Mike. This left me more amused than angered.

We arrived in Atlantic City at 12:30 a.m. I was so sleepy and ready to crash. Not James! No sooner than we checked in, he was ready to play poker. I sat at the table with him, dozing in and out of sleep. He didn't ask me if I wanted to play, so I just sat there. What the hell was I, his good luck charm? By the time 2:30 a.m. rolled around, I was through. I got up and told him I was ready to go, he could keep playing poker, but I needed sleep. He came to the room about 15 minutes after me. I made sure I was prepared for bed this time, unlike Houston when I had my boy shorts on. I was a sight to see! My hair was wrapped tightly under a scarf. I wore a bland, knee-length nightshirt over a pair of leggings. He would not be putting his hands on me this time. He got the message, and he went as far as to put a pillow in between us to show me he was going to respect me. Still, I was hanging on the edge of the bed and didn't sleep very well.

An Old-Fashioned Girl's Adventures in the Modern World of Dating

We woke up that morning, and I was so ready to go home. I was just not feeling him or this weekend. This Atlantic City trip was all about him. He was a gambler; I was not. I thought it was very selfish of him not to ask if I wanted to go to Atlantic City. He seemed to be in a great mood that morning. I spent the morning texting my cousin and informing her when we would be back in Baltimore. I asked her to pick me up at James' house so I could go and surprise my Mother. I asked James what time we would be getting back, and he said by 4 p.m. He also said he could take me to my mother's house. Oh no! That wasn't an option. I told him my cousin would be picking me up. He looked a little disappointed. Regardless, I was not introducing any man to my mother unless I was in an exclusive relationship. Before we got on the road, we had breakfast, and during the meal, James said he wanted to discuss "us."

He told me he was having a great time and really wanted us to start dating. "I can fly you out here every two weeks," he said. "Next week I would like you to come back for the Bell Biv Devoe concert." He went further to invite me to a conference in the Dominican Republic. Was I having a business meeting with him or what? I reminded James that I had a child, and my schedule was not going to revolve around him. I told James I would let him know, but I was so turned off!

Before we left he wanted to play 21 in the casino. He finally asked me what I wanted to play, and I said 21 was fine. We finally got back on the road and I was so ready to leave Atlantic City. While driving back to Baltimore he started playing some of the music we listened to on the phone after our first meeting in Miami. He was so excited. I wasn't. It was clear that I had out grown him. He asked me how long I would be at my mother's house. I told him maybe three or four hours. He told me that he had plans to take me into D.C., and then he asked if I could shorten the time I planned to spend with my mother. Oh hell no! He was really getting on my nerves now. He asked me again if he could take me to my mom's house. Maybe he was worried I wouldn't return. My cousin picked me up, and I was so happy to see her! "Damn, I have never seen you look so sad before," my cousin said when I got in the car. It was official: This man was not for me. I told her what was going on and she felt so bad. She said she and her boyfriend would come to dinner with us tonight so I would not be alone. Looking back, I probably should have just packed my bag and told him this was just not working out for me, but I felt bad because he was really trying again, for the third time. My mother was so shocked when she saw me. It was time for me to head back to James' house. I felt a little better because I knew my cousin would be in tow for dinner. When she dropped me off, James was outside waiting and smiling. My cousin saw this and said, "Damn! He's in love with you." All I could do was shake my head. While we were getting ready my cousin texted me to let me know her boyfriend did not want to drive into D.C. for dinner. I told James that we would be going to a more casual spot, and he became upset because he really wanted to take me to a nice restaurant. As we got ready to leave the house, my cousin texted again to tell me that she would not be meeting us. Her boyfriend was in one of his moods. DAMN! James looked so happy. Off to D.C. we went to an upscale establishment like James had wanted all along.

An Old-Fashioned Girl's Adventures in the Modern World of Dating

The restaurant was very intimate. I was not in the mood for this romantic evening. We ordered our food and while we waited to be served, I was shocked by what James had in store for me. It seemed as if he had been practicing his speech. He let me know how childish he was when we first met, and how sorry he was because of the way we broke up in California. He told me I had always been such a good woman, and he hated that he never saw it. He realized I was what he wanted, and he was ready to work on us getting to that place of being exclusive. He asked me to take time to think about being with him and how he thought we made a great team. He was really promoting himself. I felt like I was at a sales meeting. Damn, why couldn't I want what he wanted? Why couldn't I move forward with him? We would probably be married in a year if I just said yes, I want "us" too! But I didn't, and right then and there I realized that I was never going to be the one to settle with him, my son's father or anyone else. We left the restaurant and I was very quiet. He was excited for us to get home so we could spend the evening watching that Zoe Saldana movie, *Columbiana*. I fell asleep on the movie and woke up early, anxious to depart and go home.

James drove me to the airport ecstatic over the great weekend he thought we had. He had to see the lack of excitement on my face. As we approached the airport I was like a child getting ready to open Christmas gifts! We got out of the car, I gave him a hug and I did not look back. Once I walked inside I could see him still watching me enter the airport. I was relieved, but I still had to let him know that I was not interested in pursuing a relationship with him. I decided not to let that linger. I called him once I settled at home. He was excited to hear my voice. I told him I thought about what he said at dinner but unfortunately I did not think it would work out. He went silent for several seconds, before he finally said, "OK, cool, it's still all love and I'm glad we got to rekindle our friendship." I was so happy that was over. We hung up, and just like that, this chapter was finally over. As time went on, James called and texted a few times, but I thought it was best to pull back. Several months later, he sent me a Facebook message saying he thought we were still friends, and asking why wasn't I calling him. I never responded. He still clicks the 'like' button on some of my Facebook posts.

Update: As of this writing, James has a fiancé, and from time to time, I click the 'like' button of photos of James and this woman, who I hope will make him happy.

Chapter 4

Summertime

It was August 2013. My son was back in athletics. He plays in a sports league where nearly 98% of the parents are married. It never entered my mind that I would end up dating and falling for someone in the remaining two percent – a newly divorced parent, but it happened. His name was James 2 (By now you realize the names have been changed to protect the innocent). He caught my eye one afternoon at baseball practice. During the previous season, I could have sworn I saw a ring on his finger, but now there was no ring.

James 2 – yes, I'm with a man with the same name as my previous relationship – was tall, handsome, and something about him reminded me of my dad. We exchanged afternoon greetings and traded small talk about football. He was a Falcons fan (Which should have made this diehard Saints lover run in the other direction!) One afternoon, during one of our chats, he tried to make a bet on an upcoming Falcons-Saints game by saying, "So if the Saints win..." I didn't take the bet because I was nervous. Yes, I can be shy at times.

One afternoon toward the end of the season, he came over to my car and asked what my son's plans were for the summer. His son, who was with him at the time, smiled as I said my son would spend the summer with my mom in Maryland. He suggested that we exchange numbers to finish discussing our children's summer plans. I obliged, and the rest is history.

We spoke on the phone maybe twice before the first date. Our first date was at Chops – an upscale dining spot in Atlanta's posh Buckhead section. We met at the bar – which in hindsight should have fired off a warning in my head.

Despite this, the first date was great! I was physically attracted to him, he had a great sense of humor and a great job — he was a catch! There was, however, one concern – which at the time didn't bother me very much. He had just signed divorce papers putting an end to a 20-year marriage to his college sweetheart.

> *When a man has you sitting at the bar on your first date, he probably is not that serious about a future with you. Take note ladies. Too many distractions are taking place at the bar. Sitting at a table gives you the one on one time necessary to cultivate a relationship.*

Looking back, there was a red flag that I should have paid greater attention to. It came in the form of a conversation I had at my nail shop. I have been going to this nail shop for over 14 years. Besides getting my nails done, we also discuss my love life. When I mentioned James 2, my nail tech stopped and asked if this is the same James 2 who lived in Midtown. I confirmed that it was and she told me that one of her clients was dating him! I wanted to know every detail. She said her client traveled a lot, was really good friends with him and they started dating but she decided to give him some space since he was newly separated during the time she was dating him. I never told James 2 that I knew of this. Only in Atlanta can six degrees of separation shrink down to two!

About a week later, we went on our second date. That was quickly followed by a third that involved a decent amount of drinking and flirting. And then it happened – as the song "Are you Ready" by Fabulous played in the background, he leaned in and kissed me. Damn, James 2 could kiss! I had to control myself, especially when he asked me if I needed him to follow me home. Not yet, I thought to myself.

The next morning, he asked me to meet him for breakfast. At one point during our meal, he asked if I wanted to go to the movies that evening – wow, seeing him twice in one day! He was putting it on fast and hard, and I was loving it!

I learned that James 2 was in a fraternity. It was a fraternity I wasn't very fond of when I was in college. We went to the movies later that evening, and after the film, he asked me to come back to his house. We went back and forth for over 30 minutes of me saying no in between kissing. I finally obliged. I went home, retrieved some clothes and went to his house.

On the way, I was setting the ground rules in my head. I told myself if I was going to his house, nothing would happen, and it didn't. I was not

An Old-Fashioned Girl's Adventures in the Modern World of Dating

sleeping with him after 4 dates! Things were moving quickly after that first sleepover. I mentioned him to my friend, Dr. Hines. His exact words were, "Do not have him at the top of the list, he just got a divorce. Date other men." There was no time for other men, because I was spending all my time with James 2. Plus, truth be told, I liked the guy. I ignored my friend's advice, which looking back, was decent advice that I should have followed.

Shortly after a very romantic moment, he said to me, "April I really, really like you. It scares me because I just got a divorce. I don't want anything to change, but I just want us to have "Fun." I'm not ready for a relationship." I said OK, and

> *You must always pay attention to the words that trickle out of the mouth of the person you're dating. Listen with your head and not your heart and you will avoid having your heart broken.*

the feeling was mutual. He then went on to explain that he wanted to be selfish right now. For 20 years plus he always put his wife and child first, he didn't do anything for himself so now he was ready to do him and just have "Fun." That would prove to be a red flag I should have noticed. As the summer went on, we enjoyed an amazing chemistry, and I thought we might evolve into an exclusive relationship. He was so into me. He called me every morning on his way to work. We texted during the day, and he would call me after work.

An Old-Fashioned Girl's Adventures in the Modern World of Dating

He suggested that we go on a trip and get out of Atlanta for a little while. I was so excited! We decided to go to Turks & Caicos.

Despite seeing each other for nearly three months and enjoying many sleepovers, I held my ground and did not have sex with James 2. This was about to change. I wanted to wait until we touched down in Turks & Caicos, but the morning of the trip we made love. It wasn't the greatest, but I'll write this off to a practice round.

I was looking forward to a fun and romantic getaway, and he didn't disappoint. It was amazing, the best time I had ever had! As soon as we landed, a car service was waiting for us. He planned everything, and I loved it. He asked me to pick out the best restaurants for us to attend every night.

Not long after we arrived at our hotel we had sex again, and this time it was amazing! Holding out really does make a difference. You could say we made up for lost time. We had sex 16 times in 4 days — no exaggeration. We even did it on the beach in the hammock. If this is what a honeymoon is like, please sign me up.

We also found time for shopping, and when I saw a beautiful pair of boots that I fell in love with, he said, "That will be your Christmas present." At that moment, I thought we would have a future. I was so excited!

An Old-Fashioned Girl's Adventures in the Modern World of Dating

In addition to the obvious physical pleasure, James 2 was hitting the right spot emotionally as well. This man was becoming my dream come true!

We returned to Atlanta, and our relationship was becoming stronger. One day, I was meeting a cousin for lunch, and James 2 asked to join us.

He was interested in meeting my family, which was a good thing. Lunch was great. He wanted me to come over to his house that night. I declined, telling him that I didn't want us to get tired of each other too soon.

The next day he called me and let me know he was going to Las Vegas with a few of his frat brothers. HUH? Wait a minute! I started

> **For the fellas – If you don't want a long-term relationship, please don't ask to meet your lady's family or invite her to meet yours!**

getting a little sad because I assumed we would be spending the weekend together. Before he left, we met for dinner. I was happy he wanted to see me before his trip. I did not hear from him while he was gone, but when he returned, he texted me as he was driving back from the airport. I was happy to hear from him, and the following week we spent time together.

As the summer was winding down, my son was back in town, and we fell back into the regular school routine.

Once the school year began, we didn't see each other as much but spoke on a daily basis – 2 to 3 times a day. It was exciting seeing him at fall

An Old-Fashioned Girl's Adventures in the Modern World of Dating

baseball practice. One day, he passed me as I was walking back to the car and said, "I love your shoes." I smiled and said thank you. My shoes were these cute Prada loafers he bought me. I loved his playful side! One evening at a baseball game it started raining cats and dogs. My son and I got stuck in the bathroom area. I texted him to see if he was still at the field. He was, and he asked where we were. I told him we were stuck due to the rain. He offered to come get me and my son and take us to my car. When we got in the car, my son climbed in the back with his son. We all had to wait a few minutes to see if the rain would stop so we could continue the game. The boys were having fun on his son's iPad. I turned around and looked at them and then glanced at him. I felt comfortable in that moment. I could see a future.

In September, things started to take a turn for the worse. For the first time since we met, an entire day passed without a call. It was odd. The next morning, I called him to see if everything was OK. He did not respond until the next day. Prior to this, he had friends in town for Labor Day weekend and they spent the entire day watching college football. I didn't hear from him that entire day, but when I did get in touch with him, he seemed different following that time with his friends. His response to my text was dry, not the normal way he would respond. Things were awkward. We had made plans to see each other during the weekend, but then he backed out. He texted me to say he really didn't want to do anything and just wanted to chill. I didn't push, I said OK I understand. The following week I saw him at practice. He barely spoke. Something had changed.

The next day, toward the end of a practice session, we waited for the boys. He commented that I was acting funny. I responded, "*You're* the one acting funny!" A light drizzle fell as he shared with me what was going on with him. He went on to tell me that he was having issues with his child's mother. He felt guilty about the good time he had with me when he didn't have his son. His thoughts were all over the place as he told me he wanted to make sure he was giving his son 100%, and how he hated that his marriage failed. This left me confused, and the next few days were weird. I still didn't understand if we were still on or off. I needed answers, so I called and asked him point blank about us. He said he really liked me but he felt we were moving too quickly toward an exclusive relationship, and he was not ready for one so soon after his divorce. I asked him if he just wanted to end what we had. Were we done? Was I simply a hot summer fling? The questions made him uncomfortable. He kept saying how we had such a great time, and I was such a great woman, blah, blah, blah. I tried to hold it together, but I couldn't. I started crying; he had never heard me cry. He kept apologizing, but that made things worse. He had the nerve to say that we could go out to dinner and I could curse him out and slap him. Did he think this was a soap opera?

I kept thinking about those words from my friend who warned me not to fall hard for this guy. I also recalled James 2's own words, "I just want to have fun." The problem was I had started to fall in love with him. I was hurt badly, and what made it even worse was that I was going to run into him at my son's practices and games.

An Old-Fashioned Girl's Adventures in the Modern World of Dating

The next afternoon following the break up, I barely wanted to look at him when I saw him at practice. Another afternoon came, and I didn't see him, but I smelled his cologne. This was the worst feeling ever. About two weeks later he started reaching out to me. I was very short with him. One day, he asked me to meet him at the gas station during practice, and I agreed. We sat in the car, and he kept telling me how good I looked as he tried to hug me. I was confused, and short with him. He kept saying, "Oh it's like that?"

He saw how stand-offish I was being, and he didn't like it. After that he kept reaching out. I just wanted him to leave me alone. I saw how he was living his life on Facebook, and it hurt. Then he called me, like everything was AOK. Again, I was short with him, and he kept asking me if I would ever stop being that way with him. I was very sarcastic, trying not to fall for him again. It was November, and I remember he called and remarked how cold it was. I told him I had on my warmest coat with mink. He said, "Hmmm I bet you look great in that with some tall boots!" Huh? Was he trying to flirt, what the heck? Did he think that this feeble compliment was going to turn me on, or turn this chat into a booty call? I saw where he was going, and I just laughed at his comments and kept the conversation short.

> *For the fellas - Leave us ALONE when you end it. That shit is so confusing! Unless you have realized you fucked up and want us back, stop confusing the situation!*

An Old-Fashioned Girl's Adventures in the Modern World of Dating

He went to Arizona for Thanksgiving. He sent me a selfie, but by this time, I was cordial with him but still confused.

Fast forward to Christmas, New Year – and worst of all — Valentine's Day. At each holiday, he would send me text messages. I just wanted a clean break, but didn't have the heart to tell him to leave me alone. Deep inside I was hoping he would come back to me. Summer 2014 rolled around – one year since our first encounter – and things had not changed. I moved on and was over what could have been.

As I finish writing about him, I will tell you this: I stopped writing this book because he was the next man I had to write about. I couldn't at the time, and the book went dead. God has a funny way of showing us how strong and silly we can be at the same time. Let no man or woman, stop you from being you or reaching your goals.

I thought this book was going to end with him but guess what — God placed another man in my life, actually a few, but this last one, I promise, made me realize that what I went through with James 2 was nothing. I realized that James 2 was just not ready for what I was ready for. I don't fault him for what happened and how he ended things. I fault myself for not heeding the signs and warning.

Today, I am in a better place with him. We ran into each other at a Cirque du Soleil performance in February 2015. He was with his son. He texted me saying how good it was to see me. A part of me was still hoping. When

I got my new job in 2015, which I shared on Facebook, he reached out to me to congratulate me. He said he wanted to take me to dinner, but he never followed through with an invitation. Recently he sent me a text message saying how beautiful my Facebook photos were. My gut tells me that he is dating someone exclusively.

An Old-Fashioned Girl's Adventures in the Modern World of Dating

Chapter 5

Michael Two

We have all had moments in our lives when we find ourselves attracted to someone who shares the same astrological sign. There was a time when I dated a handful of Scorpios. None of those men are mentioned in these pages, but my dating experiences with these Scorpio men could certainly fill a second book. The chemistry is there, but after a lot of great sex, the attraction fades. Sadly, many of the Scorpio men I've dated were way too argumentative for my tastes.

Anytime I run into one now, I say "Oh no, you are not for me."

Now, back to the topic of how fate attempted to match me with men who share the same sign.

There are three men in this book who have the same sign. My son's father Michael, and a second Michael, the man you'll soon hear about in this chapter. That's right, I'm bookending this book with two men who not only share the same name, but the same astrological sign. God certainly has a funny way of working things out in our lives, and over the years, I have learned to let him lead me. Yes, it's taken time, but once you let go of what you think is best for you and let our heavenly Father lead you, life becomes a whole lot easier. (By the way, I did say three men with the same sign. I've given you two, but can you guess the third? If you ever see me or know me, just ask, and I will let you know if you are correct).

Who would have thought that I would end up dating a man who had the same name and sign as my son's father? Well it happened, and it wasn't too long ago. Of all the stories I've shared, this is probably one of the hardest to tell, and as you see how things played out, you'll understand why the story of Michael 2 – M2 for short – is so emotionally draining.

In every aspect of our lives, we learn from our mistakes, and in no area is this more evident than in affairs of the heart. This is why I was determined not to repeat the same mistakes I made with James 2 in my dealings with M2.

As I mentioned earlier, M2 was the blessing in disguise that served as the motivation to dust off and finish this manuscript (Thank you for that M2, but the check won't be in the mail).

I first met M2 at a speed-dating event in 2010. My friend and psychologist Dr. Hines decided to host an event with his girlfriend and their single friends. What a great idea, and there was a nice selection of single men! This speed-dating event occurred one year after Michael and I had broken up. I was 35, rocking bangs – a rare, drastic styling choice for me, and I was generally in a good space. I felt free, happy and excited about the possibilities ahead of me.

During the evening, Dr. Hines' girlfriend (they are now married), wanted to introduce me to men who were interested in meeting me. It was a very casual speed dating event, drinks, group conversations, and introductions.

And then I saw him — M2 — from afar. And what a sight to see! He was sooooo fine. Tall, chocolate, handsome and dressed to a 'T.' He was my type, and he wanted to be introduced to me. People always ask me, "April, what is your type?" To be quite honest, I don't have a "type." I am an equal opportunist when it comes to dating. I have dated men who were tall, short, big and small. Skin tone is not an issue either. My date choices have ranged from cappuccino to dark chocolate. However, seeing M2 made me think, that maybe I do have a "type."

I was excited but nervous. We had a nice but quick conversation because I was not trying to get locked into one man at this event.

He was a pediatrician, born and raised in Georgia. We exchanged phone numbers, and I made sure to put a star near his number.

M2 called me a few days after the event. Our conversation was very brief. He suggested that we get together for Sunday brunch. I agreed, and he also asked if I was on Facebook. We became Facebook friends, and I immediately scrolled through his pictures, the few that he had. This man was sooo damn fine, how could he not be in a relationship — especially in Atlanta? I was interested to find out his story.

We never made it to that first Sunday brunch. After that call following our first introduction, M2 never got back to me. I called once and he never got back to me (I wasn't ready to raise the red flag just yet). My first thought was he got snatched up, oh well.

About two months later one of my friends called. She was out the night before and she told me about a man she met. He was tall, a doctor, and his name was Michael. Hell no!! Again, two degrees of Atlanta separation. I told her that he was the guy from the speed-dating event I told her about who never got back to me. We laughed and screamed at the same time. I told her to go out with him. Heck, maybe I was not his type. Of course, she said no way. Now, what is funny about this is that my friend was not entirely into men like M2. She was seven years younger than me, and M2 was probably a bit too educated and professional for her at that season of her life.

She never went out with him, and neither did I until five years later — July 2015.

It was April 21, 2015 my 40th Birthday! I had planned to go to Greece and Italy to celebrate, but two of my friends couldn't make the trip, so I stayed in Atlanta and kept it very low key. I am not a big birthday person, so I was fine spending my day with myself at the Four Seasons Spa. Birthday greetings are so great on Facebook. I think we all feel special when we see all the birthday love we receive from our Facebook "friends."

An Old-Fashioned Girl's Adventures in the Modern World of Dating

It was on my birthday that I received a private message from M2. Wow!! I was shocked and surprised because he was not very active on Facebook. I had forgotten we were Facebook friends until he sent that message. It said "Happy Birthday April, I hope you're having an amazing day," with a smiley face. I was curious for a hot second why he did not post on my timeline like everyone else. I responded "thanks," and that was it.

During this time, I wasn't even thinking about a steady man. I was so happy in my new job, and I had not been on a date since September 2014. (Truth be told, in September 2014, I was actually dating two guys who both really liked me, and they both wanted to settle down. In fact, one of these guys was making travel plans for us after the first date. I was not feeling them, and it was hard to get past that little voice screaming in my head 'April, don't settle!' I was doing me!)

As the summer was in full swing, so was I. Hanging out with my friends, enjoying myself and a bit of freedom, as my son was enjoying his summer with my mom in Maryland. It was the end of July, summer was beginning to wind down and it was M2's birthday. I had planned to write on his Facebook wall, but then stopped, and instead sent him a private message as he sent me for my birthday. I sent the message, and he responded by saying how appreciative he was that I wished him a happy birthday. He also asked how I was.

I gave him an update and he ended our email conversation suggesting we keep in touch and he punctuated this with the winking smiley face emoticon.

An Old-Fashioned Girl's Adventures in the Modern World of Dating

He was clearly flirting, and it became clear why I got the private message on my birthday. I was more responsive to him this time; I guess I opened the door. I said OK, and like we did earlier at the speed dating event, we exchanged phone numbers. He was travelling out of town for work, and asked if we could get together before he left. I said yes.

We had a brief conversation before our first date, and the rest is, well, let's just say history for this book!

He suggested we meet at a local coffee shop. A coffee shop? I wondered why such an informal setting. It's not like this was a blind date. I like to bring my 'A' game to the first date, and if we were going to a nice spot for dinner I could get dressed up. That was not to be. Instead, I dressed casually for a casual date at a casual location.

Just before we met, he called to ask if I was hungry because he was starving. Instead of the coffee – as we initially planned – we met at a casual dining spot.

I arrived before him, and I guess I was looking casually cute, because two men approached me while I was waiting for him. The first one asked if he could buy me a drink, and the second one came over and asked if he could join me. I am a very loyal person, but sometimes too loyal before there is a commitment. You never know where you could meet your future husband, and sometimes we ladies put all our eggs in one basket way to soon. In hindsight, I probably should have given both men my numbers.

M2 left me waiting about ten minutes when he finally walked in. He was still as handsome as I remembered, and I was immediately attracted to him all over again. I forced myself to remain calm and not to let him see how giddy I was. We both were hungry, and we ordered right away. We ordered the same menu item. We shared similar taste in food, and this would happen quite often while we were dating.

It was a pleasant date, but when we left the restaurant, and he asked – smiling – what happened the first time we met? "You were more interested in my friend who you met two months later," were the words I wanted to say, but instead, I just laughed and smiled. He said he wanted to see me again before he went out of town. No sooner than five minutes after we went our separate ways, he texted me to say how good it was to see me, and how glad he was that we met up.

Date two was approaching a day later, and I just knew he was going to ask me to a more upscale restaurant.

See, here is the thing. I am a foodie, and M2 knew it. I even showed him the list I keep of newly opened restaurants I want to visit. When date two rolled around, it was held in another casual

Ladies, don't you love it when a man is observant enough to pick up on subtle hints?

restaurant. He knew it was a spot I visited more than 15 times. Obviously, he didn't get the hint.

Even though we would be meeting at a casual location, I still decided to wear an outfit that screamed five-star upscale. My goal was to leave him with a vision he wouldn't forget, and it worked! From the moment I got out the car and ran into him in the parking lot, he was mesmerized. He complimented me on how good I looked, fragrance and everything else a lady likes to hear.

When the hostess seated us, she commented on my shoes, and our server said, "Wow, you smell great, I like your shoes." She then told him, "You are one lucky man." He smiled, I smiled. I thought to myself, wow, if only M2 really knew and appreciated what I would give – physically, emotionally and in every way – to a man deserving of my love.

He was much more open during our second date. I learned he was once engaged to a woman who was dishonest to him. After that failed relationship, he met a woman with whom he has a two-year-old son. He admitted that he usually jumped from one relationship to the next never taking time in between to reflect on where he was, and what he wanted. In the case of his breakup with his son's mother – his relationship prior to meeting me – he had taken ample time to get his head straight. He told me it had been a year since that relationship with his son's mother, and he was ready to begin a new relationship, and ultimately get married.

He laid it all on the line. Most men don't tell you what they want upfront, so it can be a guessing game for months. I appreciated his transparency, but still, my guard was up. I shared a few details about my life, but not much more. I had grown tired of the typical second date interview. My heart had finally healed from James 2, but I was still very weary of men and their initial approach. Despite my cautiousness, the date ended on a high note!

Before we said goodnight, he asked me not to forget about him while he was out of town. He would be gone an entire month, and I told him not to forget about me either. We shared a long embrace, and it felt good. He looked at me and said he would not wash the shirt he was wearing until he returned, because he wanted to remember my signature scent. I smiled, got in my car and drove home. I could not wait for him to come back in town to see where this would lead.

One thing I noticed about M2 was that he was not a big phone person. It seemed like he loved to text. I am a talker, and I hate engaging in texting conversations. In the first two weeks while he was away, he would send me a nice inspirational text every morning. One time he did call. I was shocked, yet happy to hear his voice.

Before we continue, I'll ask that you pay close attention. If your TV is on or you have music playing, turn them off. If your kids are running around the house, go find a quiet spot and lock the door. Why? The rest of this story is going to hit you like a ton of bricks.

An Old-Fashioned Girl's Adventures in the Modern World of Dating

While M2 was away, my friend Theresa had a birthday party for her husband. It was a nice intimate celebration with a few close friends. When I arrived at the party, I recognized Theresa's friend. Her name was Meaghan, and we had met several months earlier. Meaghan and I spoke, and we immediately hit it off. We spent the majority of the evening chatting. Meaghan was so sweet. She had a nice husband, and a great sense of humor.

As the night came to a close, I noticed that Meaghan whispered to her husband Chris. She then turned to me and asked, "So, April, are you dating anyone?" I paused, sighed and replied, "Well, I actually just met this guy, who I had met years ago." I went on to say, "We had two dates that went well, but it is very early, and he won't be back for some time, so I will have to see how things progress." Meaghan smiled, and said, "Well my husband and I have a very good friend – in fact he's my husband's best friend – who we would like to set you up with, if you are open to that." After a brief hesitation, I said okay, why not? At the time I didn't know if M2 would even call me when he returned.

She grabbed her phone to access her Facebook friends. I assumed she was going to show me a picture of the man she had in mind. While she searched for the picture, she said how her husband and this guy had been friends for more than 35 years — since they were five years old! Meaghan and her husband had been married for 20 years, so it was obvious they knew him well.

An Old-Fashioned Girl's Adventures in the Modern World of Dating

As she tilted the phone for me to see this gentleman, I glanced with confusion at the image. My first reaction was, there was no way...we must just be mutual friends. Then I took a closer look – at which time, things moved in a weird combination of really fast and really slow – I pointed to make up for the words that wouldn't come out, because my jaw had dropped, which made articulation impossible.

I finally spit out the words, yelling over the party music that played in the background, "That's the guy I am dating. That is M2!"

Meaghan's eyes got wide, and then she screamed! I joined in what turned into a duet of screams as we realized I was dating her husband's best friend – the man she wanted to set me up with.

As I am writing this, I get chills flashing back to that moment. Never in a million years could I have imagined something like this would happen in my dating life. We continued screaming and then jumped out of our seats, our screams muffled as we hugged each other. Meaghan's husband – not entirely smartened up to what was happening – looked at us like we had had way too much to drink.

Meaghan finally found the words to tell her husband why we were celebrating, which immediately made his evening as he too jumped up and down. He ran outside and returned with his cell phone. He walked toward Meaghan and me and said, "You're April! M2 was just talking about you the other day. I can't believe you're the same woman!"

The story gets better. As we regained our composure, Chris told Meaghan and me that he just went outside to call M2's brother to tell him that they found M2's wife!

I could not believe that M2's best friend was telling me that I was the wife M2 was looking for! Meaghan had recently spoken to M2's brother, and they were all in agreement that they needed to find him a wife!! Everything was happening so quickly I couldn't wrap my head around what had just transpired.

Before we go further, let's do the math. M2 was chatting me up just the other day with Meaghan's husband. If that was the case, why are they both trying to play matchmaker for him? Looking back, this should have raised a red flag, but in that moment we were all too excited for me to even begin to analyze what he was saying.

It felt like I was on the business end of a flurry of Holly Holm roundhouse kicks. The first blow — M2's best friend and wife were trying to hook me up with the man I was already dating. The second foot to the

An Old-Fashioned Girl's Adventures in the Modern World of Dating

jaw — M2's best friend and wife were the godparents to Theresa, my good friend's child. Plus, Theresa and M2 were the godparents to Meaghan and Chris's child.

And the third kick — I had a reference on the man I had just been out on two dates with, and he had a reference on me. This was more than a coincidence. This was destiny…or so I thought. We finally made our way over to Theresa, to tell her the news. Meaghan simply said "Theresa, April and M2!" To which Theresa responded, "Oh yeah, why didn't I think of that. They would make a great couple." Meaghan looked at her again, and clarified with Theresa that M2 and I were dating! And then it happened all over again, we were now a trio of screams. It didn't take long for Theresa's husband to join in the chorus.

Then — seemingly on cue — I glanced at my phone to see that M2 had sent me a text that said, "So I heard you just met my best friend." As the night came to an end, Theresa and Meaghan excitedly said that we would all go out when M2 returned to Atlanta. They wanted to speed this thing up! But, wait a minute, I had to gain some control.

I asked everyone to calm down, saying it is way too early for a big group date. M2 and I had only been on two dates. Theresa looked at me, and said, "We will give you a month, then we are all going out." Meaghan then pulled me to the side looking for all of the details. She peppered me with questions. "How did you meet?" "What took so long for you all to go

An Old-Fashioned Girl's Adventures in the Modern World of Dating

out?" She even went far enough to ask, "Where were you five years ago, girl? M2's son's mother is a mess." I told her that timing was everything.

I eventually learned from Meaghan and Theresa that M2 was a great guy who just had a pattern of dating the wrong type of women. They mentioned how he had been searching for a wife and a few other comments that led me to believe that he might just be "the one."

I had turned 40, and was enjoying a new job. The thought of a new man was the icing on the cake for what was proving to be a great year.

I couldn't wait to see what was in store when M2 returned. After the big reveal with Theresa and Meaghan, the next day, M2 called. He wanted all the details. He made a comment that Meaghan had called him and said how much she liked me, and she warned him not to mess things up. I giggled and told him I looked forward to his return to the big small city of Atlanta.

When M2 returned, he contacted me and scheduled our third date. He was spending the day with his son and wanted to see me later that evening. We had yet to finalize the details of our evening when he called to cancel due to not wanting to leave his little boy's side after being away for so long. I totally understood, and he was very appreciative that I did. There is something special about dating men who have children who understand the obligation we have to our children. They depend on us. My son is my priority, and I was glad to see that M2's son was his. He sent me the cutest picture of them at the park.

A few days later, we finally had our date. We went bowling. I wore all white, and he was mesmerized. He told me he loved how pure and innocent white looked on me. We had an amazing time. I enjoyed watching him as he bowled and vice versa. At the end of the evening, we looked into each other's eyes and gave each other a quick peck. I was so nervous. Things were different now that we had mutual friends.

That date led to another and then another and another. We would spend Sundays watching football while he would get caught up on work. I was comfortable getting to know him, and over time I became more comfortable. Along the way, we shared our first real kiss. We were at the movies.

He had the best hands and he was using them to rub my thighs. After the movies, I had enough rubbing and was ready for a real kiss. I had to make sure he knew how to kiss if this was going to continue. I opened my car door, tossed my purse inside and turned back around to face him, and it was on. We kissed for a good five minutes. Yes! He could kiss, with that kiss, the deal was sealed.

Prior to our very first date, I decided that I was not going to have sex again until I was in an exclusive relationship. After James 2, I was tired of giving my body to men who just weren't worth it. Plus, it had been 2 years – yes, 2 years – since I had had sex with James 2 or anyone else. Needless

An Old-Fashioned Girl's Adventures in the Modern World of Dating

to say that when you're not getting it, you forget how good it can be. I never mentioned my abstinence with M2, but as we moved forward in the relationship, I began to see how difficult it would be to maintain my oath of celibacy.

As we continued dating, we made it a point to see each other as much as possible. M2 had his son every other week – seven days straight. The following weekend we would spend time together, and we usually saw each other once a week. M2 asked me if it was difficult to see each other during the week because we lived a good distance from each other. I told him not really and that it depended on how much homework my son had. Still, I would find at least one day a week when we could see each other. M2 also suggested that we make time for at least one lunch date a week. This was great! He was proactively initiating time for us to see each other.

As fall rolled around, and we began to settle into dating, M2 told me that Theresa invited us to a monthly dinner gathering where Chris and Meaghan would be present, and I agreed to go. It was going to be two married couples, M2 and I. I recalled one of my friends telling me that it might be too early for us to be doing group outings. He said we needed to make sure our relationship was on the right track before we started hanging out with the married folks. I told him that I understood, but this was different because M2 and I shared mutual friends.

By this time, M2 and I had sex. Yes I know, I said I was going to be abstinent until I was in an exclusive relationship. Two years was a long

An Old-Fashioned Girl's Adventures in the Modern World of Dating

time to hold out, and this was different. I had a reference on M2, I knew his people, he knew mine. He was not some random guy. Plus, at the age of 40, if I want to have sex, heck I'm going to have it! I salute you Ciara and Russell Wilson, but M2 was too damn fine for me to sit around and settle for only kissing sessions. I also felt that, eventually, our dating would lead to a relationship since that is what he told me he wanted, and his friends reconfirmed that for me.

As we got ready to attend this first group outing, I became slightly irritated with M2. It seemed as though he didn't think fast enough on his feet. On the night of the dinner party, I assumed he would pick me up, as any normal guy would do. To my surprise when I called M2, he told me he wasn't home yet. Dinner was about two hours away. I asked him when would he pick me up, and he said, "Oh, I thought we were just going to meet there." Huh? Come on Mr. intelligent doctor, why the heck would you not pick me up – especially when we had talked about you coming over after dinner. I was aggravated and called Theresa to see if I could ride with her and her husband. She stated that Meaghan and Chris — M2's best friend and his wife – were riding with them, and that it might be a little awkward but I was welcomed to ride. During this conversation Theresa asked me if I noticed how M2 tended to be a little socially awkward. I paused, thought back and told Theresa she was right! Some things M2 did were just off sometimes. I knew how super smart he was, after all he was a doctor, but then again so is Ben Carson. Now it's beginning to add up!

An Old-Fashioned Girl's Adventures in the Modern World of Dating

Back to the dinner party in a moment, but first I'd like to share one of those times when M2 really made me scratch my head. One evening he was in my home, and he was getting ready to leave. He was standing next to the powder room on the ground floor and asked if he could use the restroom. I looked at him and said yes. He then asked which one – the one upstairs or the one he was standing directly in front of! So just to see if he was kidding, I sent him upstairs – and up he went!

I recall a couple of other times when I had to take charge of a situation. Afterward, he would look at me, and say thank you. Maybe it was the country in him, or maybe it was that he really is socially awkward. One last example. M2 had an allergy to fried foods. One evening we were at an Asian restaurant, and he ordered a tempura dish. I immediately asked him about his fried food allergy. I had to educate him to the fact that tempura is fried. No, I don't expect my dates to have the culinary knowledge of Gordon Ramsay, but if you are allergic to fried foods, wouldn't you know what foods to avoid?

Back to the dinner party. That night it was raining, and I hate driving at night and in the rain. I was 15 minutes late and he was 30 minutes late. I would later learn that a topic for discussion among our friends during their ride to the party was why M2 didn't pick me up. By the time he arrived I was so aggravated. Within 15 minutes, after my second drink, I calmed down. Dinner was great, a lot of laughs, and of course the friends laying the ground rules for the monthly dinner meetings. Little did I know this was to be our first and last outing with the group.

An Old-Fashioned Girl's Adventures in the Modern World of Dating

The next day, we went to brunch and watched football all day. Despite M2's shortcomings the night before, we managed to have a great weekend. He started talking about a trip in the future once things settled down with his practice. Again, a man I'm dating talking about the future, things could only get better, or so I thought. As our dating progressed, I noticed that M2 didn't share too much about his child's mother. One evening he was upset because his son cried when he returned him to his mother. We talked briefly about it, and that was it. I also noticed that I was still holding back. Maybe I was not really over James 2.

After four months of dating, I usually start cooking for a man. However, something was not giving me that push that I had with David, or Michael. Maybe I was beginning to feel like this was not going anywhere. I have been with men, where after the second date, I'm getting flowers. After the second month, I'm being surprised with gifts, large and small. It really seemed that M2 was lacking in the fine art of dating a woman. We all want to be spoiled, and it doesn't always have to be with grand gestures. I remember James 2 giving me a beautiful piece of art. Come on M2, I'm just an old-fashioned girl. When does the courting begin? Or maybe I gave it up too fast, and he felt no need to court or maybe he really was just socially awkward.

I did decide to show off my cooking skills one morning, but when he got up, he said he had to go. Something didn't feel right in that moment. I asked him if he wanted to watch the LSU-Alabama game later that night, and he said he already had plans to watch it. I wasn't a part of those plans. The next few days were weird. It's not as if we spoke each day, but I felt like something was off. He was still consistent in sending me a good morning text daily between 9:10 and 9:30am. I was still receiving an afternoon text as well. Like clockwork, he would call me after dropping off his son and say let's get ready to watch some football. This was the first Sunday that I didn't receive a call. Something was not right. He sent me a text that day, and it was very dry. I needed to know what was going on? I called him, but he didn't answer. The next day, he sent me a text saying how sick he had been on Sunday evening. I asked him if he needed me to bring him anything, he said thanks, but no thanks. He did thank me for constantly checking on him to make sure he was OK. That week and in the days leading up to it, I knew something had changed, but I didn't know what.

We had arrived at the week before Thanksgiving. He mentioned that he was going home for the holiday. I told him that my mom was coming to town. I was under no illusions that we would spend Thanksgiving together, especially since four months of dating had passed and we were still not exclusive.

By the end of the week I knew something was not right. He would usually call or text me to confirm what we would be doing for the weekend. I took the initiative and asked him. His response was a blow that doubled me over emotionally. "Not tomorrow, maybe sometime this weekend." Ouch! Now he was treating me like some chick that was bothering him. I

An Old-Fashioned Girl's Adventures in the Modern World of Dating

purposely said, "I miss u" in the text to see what the response would be. There was none. I called Theresa, and she told me to calm down. She said everything was fine, telling me that I knew how men are when they have a lot going on. I called another friend and she said more or less the same thing. "Girl please, he is head over heels about you!" Still, deep inside I knew that my intuition was right!

I took it upon myself to send him a text message that read "I get it, you're not wanting to be bothered with me, right now, not sure why. I know you have a lot of admirers, silly of me to think there was a real interest there." While I waited for M2 to respond, I called Dr. Hines, who I had spoken to about M2 a month earlier.

When I told Dr. Hines about the changes I had noticed, he said, "April, he is not being consistent, something is not right, and you should start dating other people." Dr. Hines went on to say that when a man switches up the way he is with you, something has definitely changed. He said he didn't like the way I was sounding, and he encouraged me to keep my head up. I probably sounded tired and hopeless. If a relationship with a man who shares mutual friends with me couldn't work, then what would?

It was 5:10 p.m. on Friday, the week before Thanksgiving when M2, finally responded to my text. I told him about three weeks ago how I really didn't care for Thanksgiving anymore after my Dad had passed. I wanted this holiday to come and go! Still, M2 said how much he loved

Thanksgiving. Until you lose a parent, you really can't relate. Things were not on track to get any better when I answered M2's phone call.

I was nervous, but I already knew it was not going to be a good conversation. He sounded nervous and began the call by saying, "Hey, so I was calling to let you know what has been going on. Um, yeah, so I'm not ready for a relationship." I was silent, and he spoke again, "I just am not ready for a relationship. I thought I was." I was driving and I had to contain myself. I found the strength to respond with, "So, who mentioned a relationship yet, I didn't." He came back with, "Well, that's where it is sort of going." I thought I was on the phone with James 2. He continued, "I thought I was ready, but I'm not. I'm not over or I thought I was over my son's mother, and that relationship, but I'm just not ready to get back in one."

What M2 didn't know was that I had been told that his baby mama was crazy. So I was thinking, OK, I'm not crazy, it's been a year, what are you not over? I asked him how long has it been again since you broke up? He responded a year. I was silent and then became upset. I told him I was confused because he told me he was open to a relationship. I asked him where all of this was coming from? He was silent.

I asked him how long he had been feeling this way. He said it was about a little over a week. My intuition was right! I wanted to hang up on him and call Theresa and my other friend right away. I couldn't yet. I needed more answers. I felt that he was not being totally honest. I told him something seemed to be missing. He said "No, that's it." I asked again. He repeated that he was not ready. I wanted to scream in the phone and ask, "When the hell are you going to get over your crazy ex?" But I was calm, until he started that bullshit talk about how he liked me, what a great time we have together, blah, blah, blah.

As I pulled into my garage, I finally allowed myself to cry as the realization hit me hard. This was a relationship that ended just like the one with James 2 – four months. I felt used. Who was this "great guy" who everyone told me about? Where was his reluctance coming from and what went wrong? He heard my tears, and he said how sorry he was and he asked me not to cry. In between my sobs, I told him that I was not the type of woman who sleeps around. "I only slept with you because everyone said what a great guy you were, and you even said you were open to a relationship." I then threw a punch he was not expecting. "I had not had sex with anyone for over 2 years, 2 years!" I cried, "I would have never had sex with you if this was going to be the outcome." By this point, my head was pounding. I could barely catch my breath. He kept saying he was sorry, and then I heard a sniffle. Lawwwd was he crying too? He was so quiet, and I kept crying. This conversation lasted over 30 minutes. He finally said his battery was dying (Ha! Yeah right), and he would call me back. He never called back, and honestly, I didn't expect him to. I can only assume that he got off the phone with me to call his best friend or his brother. He mentioned to me earlier how he confided in the two of them for everything.

An Old-Fashioned Girl's Adventures in the Modern World of Dating

Following this life-changing call, I sat in the garage and didn't move for a few minutes. I called Theresa. Thank God for her being there. I always call her "busy lady." Busy lady was there for me, and I love her. I was grateful for her support in that moment. She stayed on the phone with me for an hour. She was shocked and just as confused as I was. I know she felt bad, especially when I shared that I had been abstinent for over two years until I gave myself to M2.

I did not eat that night, or the next day. The following week was up and down for me. I was still in shock. Thanksgiving came and went, thank goodness. The Sunday after Thanksgiving I received a text at 10 a.m. from M2. "Hi, how are you? I hope you had a great Thanksgiving was just thinking about you" Are you serious? I wanted to respond, "No I didn't, you ass!!" I was short. I said it was fine, and I didn't ask him about his, and that was it.

Two weeks later another text came. "Hi, how are you? I still care about u and think of u." My response, "Good. Really? Feelings are mutual." He then responded with a smiley face. I know, I know, I shouldn't have done that, but I got weak in that moment, and he was sending mixed signals. Two weeks later, "Hi, how is everything going? How is work? I don't need to come down there and handle anyone for you do I?" Was he serious? Then another text, "You look so beautiful on those Facebook pictures you posted." This man was texting me like everything is AOK. I responded. "Thanks." Then he asked me if I was ready for Christmas. I finally could not take it anymore, I responded with "Why are you texting me? It's very

An Old-Fashioned Girl's Adventures in the Modern World of Dating

confusing. You hurt me and you're texting me like everything is cool." He responded. "I wanted to know how you're doing. I still care for u." He did not say he missed me, or that he messed up. It was the "I still care for u" line that I understood loud and clear. I did not respond. On Christmas day he sent me a Merry Christmas text. I responded the same.

On January 3rd, he sent me a text after the Saints victory over the Falcons. "Awesome win," the text read. "I know u really wanted that one." I did not respond. I was finally getting over him, and I could not continue with false hope and his inconsiderate texts. Theresa was right — socially awkward!!!!

I ran into Meaghan, his best friend's wife, at an event. She was still so sweet and fun to be around. I was not sure if she was going to mention him or what happened to us. She didn't. For a quick moment I thought I was going to say something to her but I left it alone. At the event, there were a few ladies and I was the only one not married. It was fine. Believe me, I would hate to be married and unhappy. I'm not suggesting any of those ladies are, but I'm cool with listening to their stories of how they met their husbands. A few times they commented about how they could not imagine dating in this day and age. I was able to get in one comment, "Yeah, it's no fun. I'm ready to start dating white men!" They were all shocked, especially Meaghan, whose face had a look that screamed, "Well damn, my husband's best friend has pushed her to date white men!" Of course that was just all talk in the moment. I will admit that M2 left a bad taste in my mouth for black men. I had become weary and just not hopeful after dating him. This, of course, would also be temporary.

I really thought that our reconnecting was divine intervention. I was so hopeful for a possible future with him that it made me nervous and downright scared at times. I would sometimes say this is just too good to be true, but would stop myself, and say nope, He, our Father makes no mistakes, enjoy yourself April. See, it really was divine intervention. God placed M2 in my life so that I could finish this book. I previously mentioned how this book went dead after my time with James 2. Looking back, he was not a bad guy at all. He had just gotten a divorce. I didn't heed the red flag when he told me he just wanted to have fun.

M2, however, you hurt me and quite honestly, you played with my emotions during one of the most difficult times of the year for me. I had never been dumped near a holiday, and that was tough. You ought to be thankful I'm not crazy like your ex. But I thank you because I probably would not be writing this book if it weren't for you. You were the divine intervention I needed! Thank you Jesus for placing M2 in my life! You have been a great chapter, and a great addition to my book!

Chapter 6

Lessons Learned

Lessons Learned from Michael

My Son's Father, wow where do I begin?

I saw the very first red flag with him when we first started dating. I didn't hear from him for an entire month. We ran into each other a month later when he told me he had a lot going on, and that's why he "disappeared." Right then and there I should have noticed that red flag. I was 28 then. If a man tried that now, I would never give him another chance. Lesson learned. But something about him intrigued me. He treated me well after that month. He was consistent, available, and we had a great time together. Most importantly, that relationship resulted in the greatest gift of all, my son.

There's a wonderful lyric from an artist – ironically Michael introduced me to – Teedra Moses. It's a song called "No Regrets," and it truly expresses the woman I was when Michael first entered my life.

"Just a young girl ready. Didn't know what I was ready for when a feeling rained down on me that I couldn't ignore..."

Yes, it's true I have "No Regrets." I would never change a thing about the circumstances and how we met. I had never dated a man who was as financially well off as Michael. While this was very attractive, it was also a problem in our relationship. There are sacrifices you have to accept when dating a man with money. They don't always have the most structured schedule. Michael travelled a lot during the time we were together. I would find myself alone and missing him. Shopping became my man. Well guess what – that gets pretty boring after a while. I remember Michael saying once that if we ever broke up, I would have a hard time finding someone who spoils me like he did. Oh, how true those words were and are today. We all like nice things, surprises, trips and my weakness, a few Gucci bags/shoes here and there. But those material things are just that. I would rather have had him instead of those things. I would rather have had him showering me with honesty and loyalty. The old saying money can't buy you love is so true. Some women can stay and live a lie. Hats off to you! I tried and failed at that, but in my mind, I succeeded!

I would rather be free, happy and all by myself with me than to be in a one-sided relationship.

Looking back, it is clear that once he cheated on me, I never trusted him again. It is an age-old question; why do women stay in unfaithful relationships? I was never that woman who had to know her man's whereabouts 24/7, but after Michael stepped out on our relationship, I couldn't avoid the uneasy feeling that comes when you are constantly questioning your partner's fidelity.

An Old-Fashioned Girl's Adventures in the Modern World of Dating

Lessons learned from David

David, the guy I helped nurse back to health after an injury, taught me a lot. But see, it's hard to change up who you are as a person. Among other traits, I'm compassionate, helpful and loyal. So with him having an injury, it was part of my DNA to want to help him. However, I did too much too soon. Why buy the entire cow when you can get the milk for free? That, I think, has been my problem in a few relationships. I am too giving and too submissive. Also, at times I am so anxious to grab at that possibility of love that I pour myself into these men in hopes of a relationship. I'm just being me. Maybe "me" needs to be a little harder, but then that wouldn't be me. Once David realized he wanted to be with me, I was done. Once I pour all my energy and time into someone and they hurt me, it's hard for me to want to be with them again, and that is exactly what happened with David. He abused the time and nursing I did for him, then after he went to see if the grass was greener on the other side, he wanted to come back. By then it was too late. I was done, I was turned off, and I felt used.

Why put myself in a situation that might take me back to that feeling again? I have never been one to end things with someone or have them end things with me and then go back. It's scary when you put yourself out there, and you get burned. That's how I felt with David after all I did for him.

Lessons learned from James

It looks like I made a penalty on the play with this artist manager I met in Miami. I really don't go back and forth once it is over, and here we have James! I gave James another chance because we met when I was 25. By

An Old-Fashioned Girl's Adventures in the Modern World of Dating

the time he had reached out to me I was over 30, and he was close to 40. The second chance I gave James made me realize that men can mature, and they can be certain about what they want without playing games. James was just that, but I was not ready. That's why I gave him a third chance because, maybe just maybe, I was so engrossed with my team, that my focus was not where it should have been that weekend. But when that third chance came along, I came to realize that James was a great guy but just not for me. His energy level was always on 20! He was much more hyper than I was, but that is because of where he was from. I don't want to disclose where, but I will say that, at the time, I may have simply had my fill of men from that part of the country. Or maybe I was too scared to get back with James after how he treated me the first time around. Maybe something deep inside of me was scared of another bad ending. James laid it all on the line for me, stating he wanted to be with me. He messed up years ago and he saw how loving, submissive and what a good partner I would make. Damn! Now, why wasn't I ready? I recall my girlfriend looking at me like I was crazy when I told her the trip to Baltimore was a bust. She said, "Girl look at that fine man, look at that entrepreneur, what is wrong with you?" This all goes back to me not wanting to settle with a man because of my age. This all goes back to how you treat someone when you are with them the first time. I can forgive someone all day long for their actions, but it is so hard for me to bury those memories. I also think James was trying a little too hard with me, for example, liking football all of a sudden. You have to stay true to yourself in a relationship. I know I won't end up with a man who does not like sports – especially football. We will clash like James and I did the first time around. Could I

An Old-Fashioned Girl's Adventures in the Modern World of Dating

have been with James even though he didn't drink alcohol? Even though he was a pescatarian? I think so. It does, however, bring up the question how would dinner go with me cooking lamb chops for me and my son and salmon for him? These are the little things that may not seem like much but may pose difficulties in the future. Or maybe, just maybe, you're reading this, and saying I am too old to be so damn picky, and that's fine. I get it, but what I do know is that I gave James a shot the first time, and he blew it. Who knows where we could have been today, if he would have realized the type of woman I was – even as a young thing 16 years ago.

Lessons learned from James 2

Here we go – James 2, boy I really liked him!! You'll recall he caught my eye one afternoon at my son's baseball practice. I liked everything about him, his style, his look, his smartness, his playfulness, his acting skills (Yeah, I didn't disclose everything in this book), his constant communication with me. Besides my son's father, out of all the men, James 2 had the best conversation with me. I like how attentive he was and how complimentary of me he always was. However, James 2 was fresh off of a divorce. I will never forget what Dr. Hines said to me, "Put him at the bottom of your list." Maybe if I would have listened, I would not have been so heartbroken. I missed the big red flag when it was waving right in my face, when James 2 said, "I want to have fun." Duh April, of course a relationship should be fun, but you knew exactly what he meant and ignored it. I will always cherish the "fun" times James 2 and I shared. I wish him all the best with his new single life. Over 40, divorced and single could not be me. I guess that's why it has taken me so

An Old-Fashioned Girl's Adventures in the Modern World of Dating

long to find the right one. I do not want to be divorced, I want to do it just once!! Did James 2 give off signs that maybe we would be together longer than 4 months? Yes, when he mentioned he would buy a pair of boots I wanted for Christmas five months down the road. This is the time when you have to put your big girl panties on and say, "Wow, you're rolling with me until December? Great!" I should have asked him if we were still just having 'fun', but I didn't want to spoil the vibe and the moment. Sometimes, you have to spoil a moment so that you don't have to go through a bunch of spoiled feelings later down the road. Never ignore the words a man is professing to you. Be optimistic, but be smart. Listen intensely to his words and you may save yourself from potential heartbreak.

Lessons learned from Michael 2

In the beginning of this book, I mentioned how I met my son's father at the club. In the end of this book, I mentioned how I met Michael 2 at a speed dating event hosted by a mutual friend. You later learned that we both had a reference on each other from very close friends on both sides. I guess you could say no matter where you meet someone, the club, the library or through a mutual friend, there is still a great potential for heartbreak or love. At the age of 41, I will admit that dating has become a little harder. That is why I was so excited to have a reference on Michael 2. That reference enabled me to lower my guard somewhat and be more open to the possibility of this man actually being a really good fit for me. Unfortunately, Michael 2 was not my dream come true. He was a

An Old-Fashioned Girl's Adventures in the Modern World of Dating

nightmare! However, he was the nightmare that got me back on this horse – my book. For that, I'm grateful!

Always remember the adversities you have faced. I guarantee they have impacted your life for the better. Never, let a "reference" on someone change your goals or the plans you have. I had plans to stay abstinent until I was in an exclusive relationship. Did it feel like an exclusive relationship with Michael 2? Yes.

Did I think we were moving toward exclusivity? Yes. However, the bottom line was we were not, and he ran away when he knew we had pretty much arrived at the doorstep of exclusivity. I gave up a commitment to myself because I had a reference on him, and for that I fault no one but myself.

You cannot be so vulnerable that you lose sense of who you are, and what you want from the person you're dating.

In the words of my editor, (who is probably shocked reading this right now) after I submitted my Michael 2 story draft to him he said, "After I've really gone through this story word for word, I can say that Michael 2 is a real jerk." Yes, he was, but I learned so much about myself and staying true to me that I actually thank him again for being that "Jerk."

An Old-Fashioned Girl's Adventures in the Modern World of Dating

TODAY

There are so many lessons I have learned from all the men detailed in these pages. There have been many men I have dated, and I wrestled with which ones I would include in this book, but the gentlemen I have chosen are the men who have left lasting memories and growth opportunities for me.

Where am I now on this roller coaster of dating? I am still dating, still waiting patiently for "The One." I have said a million times, that I'd rather be single at 41 instead of being 41 and divorced, which is what probably would have happened had I decided to give in and settle. Yes, I have had so called options and potentials. However, I'm still waiting for that moment, that "Feeling" to come over me when "The One" has entered my life. Even though I have been through so many ups and downs in dating, not for one minute have I thought that it may never happen – marriage that is.

I believe in love, and I believe in monogamy. I believe that even a "happily ever after" will have some high and low moments. Not one of the gentlemen featured in this book has made me want to give up on love. Yes, I may have wanted to stop dating black men because of the last experience with Michael 2, but that was only temporary. I believe that love has no color. I'm open to dating men of all races. I'm open for love, today, tomorrow, and in the future to sweep me away. I am a giving, compassionate loyal woman of God, and I'm looking forward to sharing all that I have to offer, with the right one.

An Old-Fashioned Girl's Adventures in the Modern World of Dating

People always ask me "What are you looking for in a man?" I love answering that question because I finally know exactly what I want. I had walked into a co-worker's office sometime in November after things ended with Michael 2. She was replaying a sermon by Bishop Dale Bronner. The topic was "Loyalty." I walked into her office when he started breaking down four characteristics that a person with whom you are in a relationship should have – this could be a friendship, marriage, etc. He stated four traits:

- ✓ Loyalty
- ✓ Integrity
- ✓ Authenticity
- ✓ Consistency

These are four traits I have always had. I am the most consistent, loyal, authentic, woman of integrity. He went on to say that if someone you are in a relationship with is lacking one of those traits, it is time to move on. Amen, amen, amen!!

All the men I dated in this book lacked one or more of these traits:

Michael	loyalty and consistency
David	loyalty and consistency
James	consistency
James 2	consistency toward the end of the relationship
Michael 2	consistency toward the end of the relationship and authenticity

An Old-Fashioned Girl's Adventures in the Modern World of Dating

Today, because of these relationships, and realizing what they lacked in regards to what I'm searching for, I now know what I need and desire in a man for me to be happy. If I can give of myself freely, with loyalty, consistency, integrity, and authenticity, I don't think I'm asking too much of a man to do the same. Men and women, if you find yourself lacking one of those traits, it's ok, because we all are a work in progress. I just have to add one more trait to that list, a man of God, because I love the Lord!!

An Old-Fashioned Girl's Adventures in the Modern World of Dating

An Old-Fashioned Girl's Adventures in the Modern World of Dating

The One?

In December 2015 I met a man. Yes, it didn't take me that long to get back on the dating scene following Michael 2. That evening when I went out with my friend, I told her I only wanted to meet white men. Remember, I thought I was over dating black men. We met quite a few interesting characters that night. At the end of the night, my friend was speaking with a man who had a friend with him. His friend eventually came over, and my first impressions, were "Wow, he's handsome, nice style. OK, I'm back to liking black men again." He sat down next to me, and we started chatting. He was 46 years old, African-American, no children, a Morehouse grad and a successful attorney. OK, red flag alert – no children? A friend's dad told me a while ago, "If you meet a man over 35 with no children, who has never been married – something just ain't right! Beware!"

We exchanged numbers following a brief conversation. I didn't hear from him until after the new year, and that was only because his friend was going on a date with my friend. He called, well, because his friend asked my friend to go out on a date. Specifically, when Mr. Morehouse's friend told him he was going out with

Fellas - I'm really not trying to write another book, I'm trying to wrap this up, but men, please pick up the phone and call after first meeting someone. Texting is so impersonal!

An Old-Fashioned Girl's Adventures in the Modern World of Dating

my friend, I'm pretty certain the friend persuaded Mr. Morehouse to reach out to me, and he did.

Guys, don't make things so obvious. I would later find out from my friend, that he was a really nice, somewhat shy guy, and he thought I was not interested in him. I guess I was giving off that *I just don't want to be bothered with black men vibe.* Needless to say he reached out, via text. We texted back and forth a few times. He asked me if I was free. I told him I was not available due to work. I just was not going to jump on a date with him after not hearing from him for over a month. He asked me to reach out when I was free so that we could go out. Another month passed, and I had yet to reach out. Maybe I really was not over Michael 2.

It was sometime in February when he asked me out. We agreed to finally meet. The first date was great! I'm assuming that he forgot what I looked like because he kept complimenting me, and was smiling from ear to ear. Thank goodness his first date location was not casual like Michael 2. At his suggestion, we dined at an upscale restaurant, and I was able to wear a dress! When we sat down, I couldn't help to notice how nervous I was. He looked so damn good! (Michael 2 who?) Dinner and conversation were great! He was already planning our next date, and I was looking forward to it. Wow! I was happy we finally connected!

The next date was the following week, due to him travelling for work. He finally reached out via telephone, and he told me not to be a stranger. It was good hearing his voice. Date #2 arrived! We were both excited to see each other. Another great upscale restaurant. The vibe, was great, we both were on drink number two and then well let's just say things started

An Old-Fashioned Girl's Adventures in the Modern World of Dating

heating up from here – and not in a good way. He asked me the infamous question, "So, do you want more children?" "Waitress, another drink please." Uggggggggg here we go. On the second date, he was asking me a question that I think should have been asked maybe after date 5 or 6. I answered, honestly, "No, I'm done. I'm about to be 41, my son is about to be 10, I'm tired." I went on to tell him that I would be 49 when my son graduates high school. I have plans Mr. Morehouse man. Freedom! He did not like my answers. I told him, had he asked that question 3 years ago, the answer may have been different. However, at 41, there are also health risks. I just was not interested in walking around with a diaper bag at 43 or older. He obviously in that moment was not happy with me or my answers. I get it, you're 46, you have no children, and you want a child, well I'm not the one.

He went on to tell me that maybe because of me getting out of a relationship with my son's father when my son was 3, had turned me off to wanting more children. He said he understood how hard it must be for me doing a majority of things on my own. Wait just a minute smarty pants! I have many friends who are married, but feel single when it comes to raising their children. My son's father had nothing to do with this. He then started giving me examples of all his friends who had children later in life. WTF was going on? Was this man trying to convince me to have more children? This was getting more entertaining by the moment. I finally told him, that it was not easy for me to come to this decision. I told him how I was not a selfish person and always try to put myself in others shoes. If I were 41 and didn't have a child, would I still want one? At this age, I don't know if I would. I told him that I felt like my time had expired. It was time to change the conversation, this was getting way too deep for date number 2, geez!

While I do think it is important to bring to the table your wants and desires in a relationship upfront, I just thought that this being date number 2 was just a bit premature. As the night wound down, we spoke about our next date. He was the one who had to come to a decision about wanting children. He told me that he was still grappling with it, and I could tell. I don't recall how the next topic was brought up, and I still can't believe the words that were coming out of his mouth…wait for it…wait for it…. "So, I'm considering voting for Donald Trump." Huh? Laughing out loud, I said OK, stop pulling my leg, I know you're joking Mr. Morehouse man. He said it again. I thought OK, I know I had three drinks, but I'm not drunk. I told him to stop playing, and then I realized he was serious. I asked him if he was a Republican, and he responded back, "No, I'm an Independent, and I've voted for quite a few different folks."

He then went on to say, "See Trump has you all fooled, he really didn't state he is a Republican." He was serious, and it gets worse. He went on to tell me that Trump is a businessman who may be able to do something about the deficit. I nearly spit my drink out in his face. By now, I was making all sort of crazy facial expressions. He then asked why he SHOULD NOT vote for Trump. HELL NOOOOO the buck stops here. Did he think I was going to waste my breath, time and energy explaining to him why he should NOT vote for Trump? Damn, Damn, Damn. An

An Old-Fashioned Girl's Adventures in the Modern World of Dating

African-American Morehouse brother was telling me he was voting for Trump! Morehouse alums come get your boy!!!! See I have a large amount of respect for Morehouse men. They are some of the most intelligent, successful brothers I have ever met. He was ruining their legacy and the respect I had for these great men. My dad was inducted into the Morehouse College Martin Luther King. Jr., International Board of Preachers on February 27, 1992. This was, and still is a very prestigious honor. What would my dad say about this? I could only laugh on the inside and imagine. I was done, ready to go! As we walked to the valet, I couldn't wait to get in my car and call everyone I knew! We gave each other a church hug. Good night Mr. Morehouse. I have not heard from him since, thank goodness!! Maybe he realized that he really wanted to date a woman who wanted more children. Or maybe he woke up and realized that he had made a complete ass of himself professing his love for Mr. Trump. Whatever the case, I am happy that he could be the conclusion to this book. Will I settle? No! Will I continue dating? Yes!!!!

Let the fun, dating games continue, and hopefully I will encounter the one and have a new book to write about sooner than later. Until then, I'm just an old-fashioned girl enjoying adventures in the modern world of dating.

An Old-Fashioned Girl's Adventures in the Modern World of Dating